With thanks to
Jane and Christopher Coldrey

Books by Dick Francis

Blood Sport
Dead Cert
Enquiry
Flying Finish
For Kicks
Forfeit
High Stakes
In the Frame
Knockdown
Nerve
Odds Against
Slayride
Smokescreen

Published by POCKET BOOKS

Dick Francis
Smokescreen

PUBLISHED BY POCKET BOOKS NEW YORK

POCKET BOOKS, a Simon & Schuster division of
GULF & WESTERN CORPORATION
1230 Avenue of the Americas, New York, N.Y. 10020

Copyright © 1972 by Dick Francis

Published by arrangement with Harper & Row, Publishers, Inc.

ISBN: 0-671-82160-1

First Pocket Books printing October, 1978

Trademarks registered in the United States and other countries.

Printed in the U.S.A.

Smokescreen

1

Sweating, thirsty, hot, uncomfortable, and tired to the point of explosion.

Cynically I counted my woes.

Considerable, they were. Considerable, one way and another.

I sat in the driving seat of a custom-built aerodynamic sports car, the castoff toy of an oil sheik's son. I had been sitting there for the best part of three days. Ahead, the sun-dried plain spread gently away to some distant brown and purple hills, and hour by hour their hunched shapes remained exactly where they were on the horizon, because the 150 m.p.h. Special was not moving.

Nor was I. I looked morosely at the solid untarnishable handcuffs locked round my wrists. One of my arms led through the steering wheel, and the other was outside it, so that in total effect I was locked onto the wheel, and in consequence firmly attached to the car.

There was also the small matter of seat belts. The Special would not start until the safety harness was fastened. Despite the fact that the key was missing from the ignition, the harness was securely fastened: one strap over my stomach, one diagonally across my chest.

I could not bring my legs up from their stretched-forward sports-car position in order to break the steering wheel with my feet. I had tried it. I was too tall, and couldn't bend my knees far enough. And apart from that, the steering wheel was not of possibly breakable plastic. People who built spectacularly expensive cars like the Special didn't mess around with plastic steering wheels. This one was of the small-diameter leather-covered metal type, as durable as Mont Blanc.

I was thoroughly fed up with sitting in the car. Every muscle in my legs, up my spine, and down my arms protested energetically against the constraint. A hard band of heaviness behind my eyes was tightening into a perceptible ache.

It was time to make another determined effort to get free, though I knew from countless similar attempts that it couldn't be done.

I tugged, strained, used all my strength against the straps and the handcuffs: struggled until fresh sweat rolled down my face; and couldn't, as before, progress even a millimeter toward freedom.

I put my head back against the padded headrest and rolled my face around toward the open window beside me, on my right.

I shut my eyes. I could feel the slash of sunlight cut across my cheek and neck and shoulder with all the vigor of 3 P.M. on a July day at 37° North. I could feel the heat on my left eyelid. I let lines of frustration and pain develop across my forehead, put a certain grimness into my mouth, twitched a muscle along my jaw, and swallowed with an abandonment of hope.

After that I sat still, and waited.

The desert plain was very quiet.

I waited.

Then Evan Pentelow shouted "Cut!" with detectable reluctance, and the cameramen removed their eyes from the viewfinders. No whisper of wind fluttered the large bright-colored umbrellas which shielded them and their apparatus. Evan fanned himself vigorously with his shooting schedule, creating the breeze that nature had neglected, and others in the small group in the shade of portable green polystyrene sun shelters came languidly to life, the relentless heat having hours before drained their energy. The sound-mixer took off his earphones, hung them over the back of his chair, and fiddled slowly with the knobs on his Nagra recorder, and the electricians kindly switched off the clutch of mini-brute lamps which had been ruthlessly reinforcing the sun.

I looked into the lens of the Arriflex which had been recording every sweating pore at a distance of six feet from my right shoulder. Terry, behind his camera, mopped his neck with a dusty handkerchief, and Simon added to his Picture Negative Report for the processing laboratory.

Farther back, from a different angle, the Mitchell with its thousand-foot magazine had shot the same scene. Lucky, who operated it, was busily not meeting my eye, as he had been since breakfast. He believed I was angry with him, because, although he swore it was not his fault, the last lot of film he had shot the day before had turned out to be fogged. I had asked him, quite mildly in the circumstances, just to be sure that today there should be no more mishaps, as I reckoned I couldn't stand many more retakes of Scene 623.

Since then, we had retaken it six times. With, I grant you, a short break for lunch.

Evan Pentelow had apologized to everyone, loudly and often, that we would just have to go on and on shooting the scene until I got it right. He changed his mind about how it should go after every second take, and although I followed a good many of his minutely detailed directions, he had not yet once pronounced himself satisfied.

Every single member of the team who had come to Southern Spain to complete the location shots was aware of the animosity behind the tight-reined politeness with which he spoke to me and I answered him. The unit, I had heard, had opened a book on how long I would hang on to my temper.

The girl who carried the precious key to the handcuffs walked slowly over from the furthest green shelter, where the continuity, make-up, and wardrobe girls sat exhaustedly on spread-out towels. Tendrils of damp hair clung to the girl's neck as she opened the door of the car and fitted the key into the hole. They were regulation British police handcuffs, fastening with a stiffish screw instead of a ratchet, and she always had some difficulty in pushing the key round its last few all-important turns.

She looked at me apprehensively, knowing that I couldn't be far from erupting. I achieved at least the muscle movements of a smile, and relief at not being bawled at gave her impetus to finish taking off the handcuffs smoothly and quickly.

I unfastened the seat harness and stood up stiffly outside in the sun. It was a good ten degrees cooler than inside the Special.

"Get back in," Evan said. "We'll have to take it again."

I inhaled a lungful straight from the Sahara, and counted five in my mind. Then I said, "I'm going over to the caravan for a beer and a pee, and we'll shoot it again when I come back."

They wouldn't pay out the pool on that, I thought in amusement. That might be a crack in the volcano, but it wasn't Krakatoa. I wondered if they would let me take a bet on the flash point myself.

No one had bothered to put the canvas over the Mini-Moke, to shield it from the sun. I climbed into the little buggy where it was parked behind the largest shelter, and swore as the seat leather scorched through my thin cotton trousers. The steering wheel was hot enough to fry eggs.

The legs of my trousers were rolled up to the knee, and on my feet were flip-flops. They contrasted oddly with the formal white shirt and dark tie I wore above, but then the Arriflex angle cut me off at the knee, and the Mitchell higher still, above the waist.

I drove the Moke without haste to where the semicircle

of caravans was parked, two hundred yards away in a hollow. An apology for a tree cast a patch of thinnish shade that was better than nothing for the Moke, so I stopped it there and walked over to the caravan assigned to me as a dressing room.

The air conditioning inside hit like a cold shower, and felt marvelous. I loosened my tie, undid the top button of my shirt, fetched a can of beer from the refrigerator, and sat wearily down on the divan to drink it.

Evan Pentelow was busy paying off an old resentment, and unfortunately there was no way I could stop him. I had worked with him only once before, on his first major film and my seventh, and by the end of it we had detested each other. Nothing had improved by my subsequently refusing to sign for films if he was to direct, a circumstance which had cut him off from at least two smash hits he might otherwise have collared.

Evan was the darling of those critics who believed that actors couldn't act unless the director told them inch by inch what to do. Evan never gave directions by halves: he liked to see his films called "Evan Pentelow's latest," and he achieved that by making the gullible believe that step by tiny step the whole thing stemmed from his talent, and his alone. Never mind how old a hand an actor was, Evan remorselessly taught him his business. Evan never *discussed* how a scene should be played, how a word should be inflected. He dictated.

He had cut some great names down to size, down to notices like, "Pentelow has drawn a sympathetic performance from Miss Five-Star Blank." He resented everyone, like me, who wouldn't give him the chance.

There was no doubt that he was an outstanding director in that he had a visual imagination of a very high quality. Most actors positively liked to work with him, as their salaries were generous and his films never went unsung. Only uncompromising bloody asses like myself believed that at least nine-tenths of a performance should be the actor's own work.

I sighed, finished the beer, visited the loo, and went out

to the Moke. Apollo still raged away in the brazen sky, as one might say if one had a taste for that sort of thing.

The original director of the glossy action thriller on which we were engaged had been a quiet-spoken sophisticate who usually lifted the first elbow before breakfast and had died on his feet at 10 A.M. from a surfeit of Scotch. It happened during a free weekend which I had spent alone in Yorkshire, walking on the hills, and I had returned to the set on Tuesday to find Evan already ensconced and making his stranglehold felt.

There was about an eighth of the film still to do. The sly smile that he had put on when he saw me arrive had been pure clotted malice.

Protestations to the management had brought soothing noises but no joy.

"No one else of that caliber was free. . . . Can't take risks with the backers' money—can we?—not as things are these days. Got to look at it realistically. . . . Sure, Link, I know you won't work with him ordinarily, but this is a *crisis*, damn it. . . . It isn't actually in your contract in black and white this time, you know, because I checked. Well, actually, we were relying on your good nature, I suppose—"

I interrupted dryly, "And on the fact that I'll be collecting four percent of the gross?"

The management cleared its throat. "Er, we wouldn't ourselves have made the mistake of reminding you, but since you mention it, yes."

Amused, I had finally given in, but with foreboding, as the location scenes of the car all lay ahead. I had known Evan would be difficult: hadn't reckoned, though, that he would be the next best thing to sadistic.

I stopped the Moke with a jerk behind the shelter and pulled the canvas cover over it to stop it sizzling. I had been away exactly twelve minutes, but when I walked round into the shelter Evan was apologizing to the camera crews for my keeping them hanging around in this heat. Terry made a disclaiming gesture, as I could see perfectly well that he had barely finished loading the Arriflex with a fresh magazine out of the icebox. No one bothered to argue. At a hundred degrees in the shade, no one but Evan had any energy.

"Right," he said briskly. "Get into the car, Link. Scene 623, Take 10. And let's for hell's sake get this one right."

I said nothing. Of the nine previous takes, three had been fogged; that left today's six, and I knew, as everyone else knew, that Evan could have used any one of them.

I got into the car. We retook the scene twice more.

Evan managed to shake his head dubiously even after that, but the head cameraman told him the light was getting too yellow, and even if they took any more it would be no good, as they wouldn't be able to match it to the scene that went before. Evan gave in only because he could come up with no possible reason for going on, for which Apollo had my thanks.

The unit packed up. The girl came limply across and undid the handcuffs. Two general duty men began to wrap up the Special in dust sheets and pegged-down tarpaulins, and Terry and Lucky dismantled their cameras and packed them in cases, to take them away for the night.

In twos and threes, everyone straggled across to the caravans, with me driving Evan in the Moke and saying not a word to him on the way. The coach had arrived from the small nearby town of Madroledo, bringing the two night watchmen. "Coach" was a flattering word for it: an old airport runabout bus, with a lot of room for equipment and minimum comfort for passengers. The company said they had stipulated a luxury touring coach with air conditioning, but the bone-shaker was what had actually turned up.

The hotel in Madroledo where the whole unit was staying was in much the same category. The small inland town, far from the tourist beat, offered amenities that package-holiday operators would have blanched at; but the management had had to install us there, they said, because the best hotels on the coast at Almería were booked solid by hundreds of Americans making an epic Western in the next bit of desert to ours.

In fact, I much preferred even the rough bits of this film to the last little caper I had been engaged on, a misty rock-climbing affair in which I had spent days and days clinging to ledges while the effects men showered buckets of artificial rainstorm over my head. It was never much good my complaining about the occasional wringers I got put through: I'd started out as a sort of stunt man, they said, so what was a little cold, a little heat? Get out there on the ledges, they said. Get out there in the car. And just concentrate on how much lolly you're stacking away to comfort you later through arthritis. Never fear, they said, we won't let you come to any real harm—not so long as the insurance premiums are so high, and not so long as almost every film you make covers its production costs in the first month of showing. Such charming people, those managements, with dollar signs for eyes, cash registers for hearts.

Cooler and cleaner, the entire unit met for before-dinner drinks in Madroledo's idea of an American bar. Away out on the plain in the warm night, the Special sat under its guarding floodlights, a shrouded hump, done with for the day. By tomorrow night, I thought, or at least the day after, we would have completed all the scenes which needed me stuck in the driving seat. Provided Evan could think of no reason for reshooting Scene 623 yet again, we only had 624 and 625 to do, the cavalry-to-the-rescue bits. We had done Scenes 622 and 621, which showed the man waking from a drugged sleep and assessing his predicament, and the helicopter shots were also in the can: the wide-circling and then narrowing aerial views which established the Special in its bare lonely terrain, and gave glimpses of the man slumped inside. Those were to be the opening shots of the film and the background to the credits, the bulk of the story being told afterward in one long flashback to explain why the car and the man were where they were.

In the bar, Terry and the Director of Photography were holding a desultory discussion about focal lengths, punctuating every wise thought with draughts of *sangría*. The

Director, otherwise known professionally as the lighting cameraman, and personally as Conrad, patted me gently on the shoulder and pressed an almost cold glass into my hand. We had all grown to like this indigenous thirst quencher, a rough red local wine diluted by ice and a touch of the fruit salads.

"There you are, dear boy; it does wonders for the dehydration," he said, and then in the same breath finished his broken-off sentence to Terry. "So he used an eighteen-millimeter wide-angle and of course every scrap of tension evaporated from the scene."

Conrad spoke from the strength of an Oscar on the sideboard, and called everyone "dear boy," from chairmen downward. Aided by a naturally resonant bass voice and a droopy cultivated mustache, he had achieved the notable status of "a character" in a business which specialized in them, but behind the flamboyance there was a sharp technician's mind which saw life analytically at twenty-four frames per second and thought in Eastman Color.

Terry said, "Beale Films won't use him now because of the time he shot two thousand feet one day at Ascot without an eighty-five filter, and there wasn't another race meeting due there until a month after they ran into compensation time. . . ."

Terry was fat, bald, forty, and had given up earlier aspirations to climb to Director of Photography with his name writ large in credits. He had settled instead for being a steady, reliable, experienced, and continually in-work craftsman, and Conrad always liked to have him on his team.

Simon joined us and Conrad gave him, too, a glass of *sangría*. Simon, the clapper-loader of Terry's crew, had less assurance than he ought to have had at twenty-three, and was sometimes naïve to the point where one speculated about arrested development. His job entailed operating the clapper board before every shot, keeping careful records of the type and footage of film used, and loading the raw film into the magazines which were used in the cameras.

Terry himself had taught him how to load the magazines, a job which meant winding unexposed film onto reels, in total darkness and by feel only. Everyone, to begin with, learned how to do it with unwanted exposed film in a well-lit room, and practiced it over and over until he could do it with his eyes shut. When Simon could do this faultlessly, Terry sent him to load some magazines in earnest, and it was not until after a long day's shooting that the laboratory discovered all the film was completely black.

Simon, it appeared, had done exactly what he had been taught: gone into the loading room and threaded the film onto the magazine with his eyes shut. And left the electric light on while he did it.

He took a sip of his pink restorer, looked at the others in bewilderment, and said, "Evan told me to write 'print' against every one of those shots we took today." He searched their faces for astonishment and found none. "But, I say," he protested, "if all the first takes were good enough to print, why on earth did he go on doing so many?"

No one answered except Conrad, who looked at him with pity and said, "Work it out, dear boy. Work it out." But Simon hadn't the equipment.

The barroom was large and cool, with thick white painted walls and a brown tiled floor: pleasant in the daytime, when we were seldom there, but too stark at night because of the glaring striplighting some insensitive soul had installed on the ceiling. The four girls, sitting languidly round a table with half-empty glasses of lime juice and Bacardi and soda, took on a greenish tinge as the sunlight faded outside, and aged ten years. The pouches beneath Conrad's eyes developed shadows, and Simon's chin receded too far for flattery.

Another long evening stretched ahead, exactly like the nine that had gone before: several hours of shop and gossip punctuated by occasional brandies, cigars, and a Spanish-type dinner. I hadn't even any lines to learn for the next day, as my entire vocal contribution to Scenes 624 and 625 was to be a variety of grunts and mumbles. I would be glad, I thought, by God I would be glad, to get back home.

We went in to eat in a private dining room as uninviting as the bar. I found myself between Simon and the handcuffs girl, two-thirds of the way along one side of the long table at which we all sat together haphazardly. About twenty-five of us, there were: all technicians of some sort except me and the actor due to amble to the rescue as a Mexican peasant. The group had been cut to a minimum, and our stay scheduled for as short a time as possible; the management had wanted even the desert scenes shot at Pinewood like the rest of the film, or at least on some dried-up bit of England, but the original director had stuck out for the authentic shimmer of real heat, damn and bless his departed spirit.

There was an empty space around the far side of the table.

No Evan.

"He's telephoning," the handcuffs girl said. "I think he's been telephoning ever since we came back."

I nodded. Evan telephoned the management most evenings, though not normally at great length. He was probably having difficulty getting through.

"I'll be glad to go home," the girl said, sighing. Her first location job, which she had looked forward to, was proving disappointing: boring, too hot, and no fun. Jill—her real name was Jill, though Evan had started calling her Handcuffs, and most of the unit had copied him—slid a speculative look sidewise at my face, and added, "Won't you?"

"Yes," I said neutrally.

Conrad, sitting opposite, snorted loudly. "Handcuffs, dear girl, that's cheating. Anyone who prods him has her bet canceled."

"It wasn't a prod," she said defensively.

"Next best thing."

"Just how many of you are in this pool?" I asked sarcastically.

"Everyone except Evan," Conrad admitted cheerfully. "Quite a healthy little jackpot, it is."

"And has anyone lost their money yet?"

Conrad chuckled. "Most of them, dear boy. This afternoon."

"And you," I said, "have you?"

He narrowed his eyes at me and put his head on one side. "You've a temper that blows the roof off, but usually on behalf of someone else."

"He can't answer your question, you see," Jill explained to me. "That's against the rules, too."

But I had worked with Conrad on three previous films, and he had indeed told me where he had placed his bet.

Evan came back from telephoning, walked purposefully to his empty chair, and splashed busily into his turtle soup. Intent, concentrated, he stared at the table and either didn't hear or didn't wish to hear Terry's tentative generalities.

I looked at Evan thoughtfully. At forty he was wiry, of medium height, and packed with aggressive energy. He had undisciplined black curling hair, a face in which even the bones looked determined, and fierce hot brown eyes. That evening the eyes were looking inward, seeing visions in his head; and the tumultuous activity going on in there showed unmistakably in the tension in his muscles. His spoon was held in rigid fingers, and his neck and back were as stiff as stakes.

I didn't like his intensity, not at any time or in any circumstance. It always set up in me the unreasonable reaction of wanting to avoid doing what he was pressing for, even when his ideas made good sense. That evening he was building up a good head of steam, and my own antipathy rose to match.

He shoveled his way briskly through the Anglicized paella which followed, and pushed his empty plate away decisively.

"Now . . ." he said, and everybody listened. His voice sounded loud and high, strung up with his inner urgency.

It would have been impossible to sit in that room and ignore him.

"As you know, this film we are making is called *Man in a Car*."

We knew.

"And as you know, the car has figured in at least half the scenes that have been shot."

We knew that, too, better than he did, as we had been with it all through.

"Well . . ." He paused, looking round the table, collecting eyes. "I have been talking to the producer, and he agrees. . . . I want to change the emphasis—change the whole shape of the film. There are going to be a number of flashbacks now, and not just one. The story will jump back every time from the desert scene, and each desert shot will give an impression of the days passing, and show the man growing weaker. There is to be no rescue, as such. This means, I'm afraid, Stephen"—he looked directly at the other actor—"that your part is out entirely, but you will of course be paid what was agreed." He turned back to the unit in general. "We are going to scrap those cool witty scenes of reunion with the girl that you did at Pinewood. Instead, we will end the film with the reverse of the opening. That is to say, a helicopter shot that starts with the car in close-up and gradually recedes from it until it is merely a dot on the plain. The view will widen just at the end to indicate a peasant walking along a ridge of hill, leading a donkey, and everyone who sees the film can decide for himself whether the peasant rescues the man or passes by without seeing him."

He cleared his throat into a wholly attentive silence. "This of course means that we shall have to do much more work here on location. I estimate that we will be here for at least another two weeks, as there will have to be many more scenes of Link in the car."

Someone groaned. Evan looked fiercely in the direction of the protest and silenced it effectively. Only Conrad made any actual comment.

"I'm glad I'm behind the camera, and not in front of

it," he said slowly. "Link's showing wear and tear already."

I pushed the last two bits of chicken around with my fork, not really seeing my plate. Conrad was staring across at me; I could feel his eyes. And all the others', too. It was the actor in me, I knew, that kept them waiting while I ate a mouthful, drank some wine, and finally looked up again at Evan.

"All right," I said.

A sort of quiver ran through the unit, and I realized they had been holding their breath for the explosion of the century. But, setting my own feelings aside, I had to admit that what Evan had suggested made excellent film sense, and I trusted to that instinct, if not to his humanity. There was a lot I would do to make a good film.

He was surprised at my unconditional agreement, but also excited by it. Visions poured out of him, faster than his tongue.

"There will be tears—and skin cracks, and sun blisters—and terrible thirst—and muscles and tendons quivering with strain like violin strings, and hands curled with cramp—and agony and frightful despair—and the scorching, inexorable, thunderous silence—and towards the end, the gradual disintegration of a human soul, so that even if he is rescued he will be different. And there won't be a single person who sees the film who doesn't leave exhausted and wrung out and filled with pictures he'll never forget."

The camera crews listened with an air of we've-seen-all-this-before and the make-up girl began looking particularly thoughtful. It was only I who seemed to see it from the inside looking out, and I felt a shudder go through my gut as if it were a real dying I was to do, and not pretense. It was foolish. I shook myself; shook off the illusion of personal involvement. To be any good, acting had to be deliberate, not emotional.

He paused in his harangue, waiting with fixed gaze for me to answer him, and I reckoned that if I were not to let

him stampede all over me it was time to contribute something myself.

"Noise," I said calmly.

"What?"

"Noise," I repeated. "He would make a noise, too, at
first. Shouting for help. Shouting from fury, and hunger,
and terror. Shouting his bloody head off."

Evan's eyes widened and embraced the truth of it.

"Yes," he said. He took a deep ecstatic breath at the
thought of his idea taking actual shape. "Yes."

Some of the inner furnace died down to a saner, more
calculating heat.

"Will you do it?" he said.

I knew he meant not would I just get through the
scenes somehow, but would I put into them the best I
could. And he might well ask, after his behavior to me
that day. I would, I thought; I would make it bloody marvelous, but I answered him flippantly.

"There won't be a dry eye in the house."

He looked irritated and disappointed, which would do
no harm. The others all relaxed and began talking, but
some undercurrent of excitement had awakened, and it
was the best evening we had since we arrived.

So we went back to the desert plain for another two
weeks, and it was lousy, but the glossy little adventure
turned into an eventual box-office blockbuster which even
the critics seemed to like.

I got through the whole fortnight with my temper in-
tact; and in consequence Conrad, who had guessed right,
won his bet and scooped the pool.

2

England in August seemed green and cool in comparison when I got back. At Heathrow I collected my car, a production-line B.M.W., darkish blue, ordinarily jumbled registration number, nothing Special about it, and drove westward into Berkshire with a feeling of ease.

Four o'clock in the afternoon.

Going home.

I found myself grinning at nothing in particular. Like a kid out of school, I thought. Going home to a summer evening.

The house was middle-sized, part old, part new, built on a gentle slope outside a village far up the Thames. There was a view down over the river, and lots of evening sun, and an unsignposted lane to approach by that most people missed.

There was a boy's bicycle lying half on the grass, half on the drive, and some gardening tools near a half-weeded flower bed. I stopped the car outside the garage, looked at the shut front door, and walked round the house to the back.

I saw all four of them before they saw me: like looking

in through a window. Two small boys splashing in the pool with a black-and-white beach ball. A slightly faded sun umbrella nearby, with a little girl lying on an air bed in its shade. A young woman with short chestnut hair, sitting on a rug in the sun, hugging her knees.

One of the boys looked up and saw me standing watching them from across the lawn.

"Hey," he shouted. "Dad's home," and ducked his brother.

I walked toward them, smiling. Charlie unstuck herself from the rug and came unhurriedly to meet me.

"Hi," she said. "I'm covered in oil." She put her mouth forward for a kiss and held my face between the insides of her wrists.

"What on earth have you been doing with yourself?" she asked. "You look terribly thin."

"It was hot in Spain," I said. I walked back to the pool beside her, stripping off my loosened tie, and then my shirt.

"You didn't get very sunburned."

"No. Sat in the car most of the time."

"Did it go all right?"

I made a face. "Time will tell. How are the kids?"

"Fine."

I had been away a month. It might have been a day. Any father coming home to his family after a day's work.

Peter levered himself out of the pool via his stomach and splashed across the grass.

"What did you bring us?" he demanded.

"Pete, I've *told* you," Charlie said exasperated, "if you ask, you won't *get*."

"You won't get much this time, anyway," I told him. "We were miles from any decent shops. And go and pick your bike up off the drive."

"Oh, honestly," he said. "The minute you're home, we've done something wrong." He retreated round the house, his back view stiff with protest.

Charlie laughed. "I'm glad you're back."

"Me, too."

"Dad, look at me. Look at me do this, Dad."

I obediently watched while Chris turned some complicated sort of somersault over the beach ball and came up with a triumphant smile, shaking water out of his eyes and waiting for praise.

"Jolly good," I said.

"Watch me again, Dad."

"In a minute."

Charlie and I walked over to the umbrella, and looked down at our daughter. She was five years old, brown-haired, and pretty. I sat down beside the air bed and tickled her tummy. She chuckled, and smiled at me deliciously.

"How's she been?"

"Same as usual."

"Shall I take her in the pool?"

"She came in with me this morning . . . but she loves it. It wouldn't do her any harm to go again."

Charlie squatted down beside her. "Daddy's home, little one," she said. But to Libby, our little one, the words themselves meant almost nothing. Her mental development had slowed to a snail's pace after the age of ten months, when her skull had been fractured. Peter, who had been five then, had lifted her out of her pram, wanting to be helpful and bring her indoors for lunch. But Charlie, going out to fetch her, had seen him trip and fall, and it had been Libby's head which struck the stone step on the terrace of the flat we then occupied in London. The baby had been stunned, but after an hour or two the doctor could find nothing wrong with her.

It was only two or three weeks later that she fell sick, and later still, when she was surviving a desperate illness, that the hospital doctors told us she had had a hairline fracture at the base of the brain, which had become infected and given her meningitis. We were so relieved that she was alive that we scarcely took notice of the cautiously phrased warnings. "We must not be surprised if she is a little late in developing." Of course she would be a little late after being so ill. But she would soon catch up, wouldn't she? And we dismissed the dubious expression, and that unfamiliar word "retarded."

During the next year, we had learned what it meant and, in facing such a mammoth disaster, had also discovered much about ourselves. Before the accident, our marriage had been shaking toward disintegration under the onslaughts of prosperity and success; after it, we had gradually cemented ourselves together again, with a much clearer view of what was really important and what was not.

We had left the bright lights, the adulation, and the whoopee, and gone to live in the country, where both of us had our original roots, anyway. Better for the kids, we said; and knew it was better for us, too.

Libby's state no longer caused us any acute grief. It was just part of life, accepted and accustomed. She was treated with good humor by the boys, with love by Charlie, and with gentleness by me; and as she was seldom ill and seemed to be happy enough, it could have been a lot worse.

It had proved harder in the end to grow skins against the reactions of strangers, but after all these years neither Charlie nor I gave a damn what anyone said. So maybe Libby couldn't talk yet, couldn't walk steadily, fed herself messily, and was not reliably continent, but she was our daughter, and that was that.

I went into the house, changed into swimming trunks, and took her with me into the pool. She was slowly learning to swim, and had no fear of the water. She splashed around happily in my grasp, patted my face with wet palms and called me "Dada," and wound her arms round my neck and clung to me like a little limpet.

After a bit, I handed her over to Charlie to dry, and played water polo (of sorts) with Peter and Chris, and after twenty minutes of that decided that even Evan Pentelow was a lesser taskmaster.

"More, Dad," they said, and, "I *say,* Dad, you aren't getting out already, are you?"

"Yes," I said firmly, and dried myself sitting beside Charlie on the rug.

She put the kids to bed while I unpacked, and I read them stories while she cooked, and we spent the evening by ourselves, eating chicken and watching an old movie (from before my days) on television. After that we stacked the dishes in the washer and went to bed.

We had no one else living in the house with us. On four mornings a week, a woman walked up from the village to help with the chores, and there was also a retired nurse there who would always come to look after Libby and the boys if we wanted to go out. These arrangements were Charlie's own choice: I had married a quiet, intelligent girl who had grown into a practical, down-to-earth, and—to her own surprise—domesticated woman. Since we had left London, she had developed an added strength which one could only call serenity, and although she could on occasion lose her temper as furiously as I could, her foundations were now built on rock.

A lot of people in the film world, I knew, thought my wife unexciting and my home life a drag, and expected me to break out in blondes and redheads, like a rash. But I had very little in common with the sort of larger-than-life action man I played in film after film. The films were my work, and I worked hard at them, but I didn't take them home.

Charlie snuggled beside me under the duvet and put her head on my chest. I smoothed my hands over her bare skin, feeling the ripple deep in her abdomen and the faint tremble in her legs.

"O.K.?" I asked, kissing her hair.

"Very . . ."

We made love in the simple, ordinary way, as we always did; but because I had been away a month it was one of the best times, one of the breath-taking, fundamental, indescribable times which became a base to live from. Certainty begins here, I thought. With this, what else did one need?

"Fantastic," Charlie sighed. "That was *fantastic*."

"Remind us to do it less often."

She laughed. "It does improve with keeping."

"Mm." I yawned.

"I say," she said, "I was reading a magazine in the dentist's waiting room this morning while Chris was having his teeth done, and there was a letter in it on the sob-stuff page, from a woman who had a bald fat middle-aged husband she didn't fancy, and she was asking for advice on her sex life. And do you know what advice they gave her?" There was a smile in her voice. "It was 'Imagine you are sleeping with Edward Lincoln.'"

"That's silly." I yawned again.

"Yeah. . . . Actually, I thought of writing and asking what advice they would give *me*."

"Probably tell you to imagine you're sleeping with some fat bald middle-aged man you don't fancy."

She chuckled. "Maybe I will be, in twenty years' time."

"You are so kind."

"Think nothing of it."

We drifted contentedly to sleep.

I had a race horse, a steeplechaser, in training with a thriving stable about five miles away, and I used to go over when I was not working and ride out with the string at morning exercise. Bill Tracker, the energetic trainer, did not in general like to have owners who wanted to ride their own horses, but he put up with my intermittent presence on the same two counts that his stable lads did; namely, that my father had once been a head lad along in Lambourn, and that I had also at one time earned my living by riding, even if not in races.

There wasn't much doing in August, but I went over, a couple of days after my return, and rode out on the Downs. The new jumping season had barely begun, and most of the horses, including my own, were still plodding round the roads to strengthen their legs. Bill generously let me take out one of the more forward hurdlers, which was due to have its first run in two weeks or so, and as usual I much appreciated the chance he gave me to ride to some useful purpose, and to shake the dust off the one skill I had been born with.

I had learned to ride before I could walk, and had grown up intending to be a jockey. But the fates weren't kind: I was six feet tall when I was seventeen, and whatever special something it took to be a racer, I hadn't got. The realization had been painful; the switch to jigging along in films a wretched second best.

Ironic, to remember that.

The Downs were wide and windy and covered in breathable air: nice and primeval still, except for the power station on the horizon and the distant slash of a motorway. We walked and trotted up to the gallops, cantered, galloped where and when bidden, and walked down again, cooling the horses off; and it was absolutely great.

I stayed to breakfast with the Trackers and rode my own horse afterward with the second lot round the roads, cursing like the rest of the lads at the cars which didn't slow down to pass. I relaxed easily in the saddle and smiled as I remembered how my father had yelled himself hoarse at me—"Sit *up,* you bloody boy! And keep your elbows *in.*"

Evan Pentelow and Madroledo were in another world.

When I got back, the boys were squabbling noisily over whose turn it was with the unbroken roller skates, and Charlie was making a cake.

"Hi," she said. "Did you have a good ride?"

"Great."

"Fine. . . . Well, there weren't any calls, except Nerissa rang. Will you two be *quiet;* we can't hear ourselves think."

"It's *my* turn," Peter yelled.

"If you two don't shut up, I'll twist your ears," I said.

They shut up. I'd never carried out the often repeated threat, but they didn't like the idea of it. Chris immediately pinched the disputed skates and disappeared out of the kitchen, and Peter gave chase with muted yells.

"Kids!" Charlie said disgustedly.

I scooped out a fingerful of raw cake mixture and got my wrist slapped.

"What did Nerissa want?"

"She wants us to go to lunch." Charlie paused, with the wooden spoon dropping gouts of chocolate goo into the bowl. "She was a bit—well—odd, in a way. Not her usual brisk self. Anyway, she wanted us to go today."

"Today!" I said, looking at the clock.

"Oh, I told her we couldn't, that you wouldn't be back until twelve. So she asked if we could make it tomorrow."

"Why the rush?"

"Well, I don't know, darling. She just said could we come as soon as poss. Before you got tied up in another film, she said."

"I don't start the next one until November."

"Yes, I told her that. Still, she was pretty insistent. So I said we'd love to go tomorrow unless you couldn't, in which case I'd ring back this lunchtime."

"I wonder what she wants," I said. "We haven't seen her for ages. We'd better go, don't you think?"

"Oh, yes, of course."

So we went.

It is just as well one can never foresee the future.

Nerissa was a sort of cross between an aunt, a godmother, and a guardian, none of which I had ever actually had. I had had a stepmother who loved her own two children exclusively, and a busy father nagged by her to distraction. Nerissa, who had owned three horses in the yard where my father reigned, had given me first sweets, then pound notes, then encouragement, and then, as the years passed, friendship. It had never been a close relationship, but always a warmth in the background.

She was waiting for us, primed with crystal glasses and a decanter of dry sherry on a silver tray, in the summer sitting room of her Cotswold house, and she rose to meet us when she heard her manservant bringing us through the hall.

"Come in, my dears, come in," she said. "How lovely

to see you. Charlotte, I love you in yellow . . . and, Edward, how very thin you are."

She had her back to the sunlight which poured in through the window framing the best view in Gloucestershire, and it was only when we each in turn kissed her offered cheek that we could see the pitiful change in her.

The last time I had seen her, she had been an attractive woman of fifty plus, with young blue eyes and an apparently indestructible vitality. Her walk seemed to be on the edge of dancing, and her voice held a wise sense of humor. She came from the blue-blooded end of the Stud Book and had what my father had succinctly described as "class."

But now, within three months, her strength had vanished and her eyes were dull. The gloss on her hair, the spring in her step, the laugh in her voice: all were gone. She looked nearer seventy than fifty, and her hands trembled.

"Nerissa," Charlie exclaimed in a sort of anguish, for she, like me, held her in much more than affection.

"Yes, dear. Yes," Nerissa said comfortingly. "Now sit down, dear, and Edward shall pour you some sherry."

I poured all three of us some of the fine pale liquid, but Nerissa hardly sipped hers at all. She sat in a gold brocade chair in a long-sleeved blue linen dress, with her back to the sun and her face in shadow.

"How are those two little monkeys?" she asked. "And how is dear little Libby? And Edward, my dear, being so thin doesn't suit you." She talked on, making practiced conversation and looking interested in our answers, and gave us no opening to ask what was the matter with her.

When she went into the dining room, it was with the help of a walking stick and my arm, and the feather-light lunch which had been geared to her needs did nothing to restore my lost pounds. Afterward, we went slowly back to the summer room for coffee.

"Do smoke, Edward, dear. There are some cigars in the cupboard. You know how I love the smell . . . and so few people smoke here nowadays."

I imagined they didn't because of her condition, but if she wanted it, I would, even though I rarely did, and only in the evening. They were Coronas, but a little dry from old age. I lit one, and she inhaled the smoke deeply and smiled with real pleasure.

"That's so good," she said.

Charlie poured the coffee, but again Nerissa hardly drank. She settled back gently into the same chair as before, and crossed her elegant ankles.

"Now, my dears," she said calmly, "I shall be dead by Christmas."

We didn't even make any contradictory noises. It was all too easy to believe.

She smiled at us. "So sensible, you two are. No silly swooning, or making a fuss." She paused. "It appears I have some stupid ailment, and they tell me there isn't much to be done. As a matter of fact, it's what they *do* do which is making me feel so ill. Before, it wasn't so bad . . . but I have had to have X rays so often . . . and now all these horrid cytotoxic drugs, and really they make me most unwell." She managed another smile. "I've asked them to stop, but you know what it's like. If they can, they say they must. Quite an unreasonable view to take, don't you think? Anyway, my dears, that need not trouble you."

"But you would like us to do something for you?" Charlie suggested.

Nerissa looked surprised. "How did you know I had anything like that in mind?"

"Oh . . . because you wanted us in a hurry—and you must have known for weeks how ill you were."

"Edward, how clever your Charlotte is," she said. "Yes, I do want something . . . I want Edward to do something for me, if he will."

"Of course," I said.

A dry amusement crept back into her voice. "Wait until you hear what it is before you promise so glibly."

"O.K."

"It is to do with my horses." She paused to consider,

her head inclined to one side. "They are running so badly."

"But," I said in bewilderment, "they haven't been out yet this season."

She still had two steeplechasers trained in the yard where I had grown up, and although since my father's death I had had no direct contact with them, I knew they had won a couple of races each the season before.

She shook her head. "Not the jumpers, Edward. My other horses. Five colts and six fillies, running on the flat."

"On the flat? I'm sorry . . . I didn't realize you had any."

"In South Africa."

"Oh." I looked at her a bit blankly. "I don't know anything about South African racing. I'm awfully sorry. I'd love to be of use to you, but I don't know enough to begin to suggest why your horses there are running badly."

"It's nice of you, Edward, dear, to look disappointed. But you really can help me, you know. If you will."

"Just tell him how," Charlie said, "and he'll do it. He'll do anything for you, Nerissa."

At that time, and in those circumstances, she was right. The finality of Nerissa's condition made me sharply aware of how much I had always owed her: not in concrete terms as much as in the feeling that she was *there*, interested and caring about what I did. In my motherless teens, that had meant a lot.

She sighed. "I've been writing to my trainer out there about it, and he seems very puzzled. He doesn't know why my horses are running badly, because all the others he trains are doing all right. But it takes so long for letters to pass—the postal services at both ends seem to be so erratic these days. And I wondered, Edward, my dear, if you could possibly . . . I mean, I know it's a good deal to ask, but could you possibly give me a week of your time, and go out there and find out what's happening?"

There was a small silence. Even Charlie did not rush to say that of course I would go, although it was clear already that it would have to be a matter of how, not whether.

Nerissa went on persuasively, "You see, Edward, you do know about racing. You know what goes on in a stable, and things like that. You could see, couldn't you, if there is something wrong with their training? And then of course you are so good at investigating things."

"I'm what?" I asked. "I've never investigated anything in my life."

She fluttered a hand. "You know how to find things out, and nothing ever deflects you."

"Nerissa," I said suspiciously, "you've been seeing my films."

"Well, of course. I've seen nearly all of them."

"Yes, but that's not me. Those investigating supermen, they're just acting."

"Don't be silly, Edward, dear. You couldn't do all the things you do in films without being brave and determined and very clever at finding things out."

I looked at her in a mixture of affection and exasperation. So many people mistook the image for the man, but that she should . . .

"You've known me since I was eight," I protested. "You know I'm not brave or particularly determined. I'm ordinary. I'm me. I'm the boy you gave sweets to when I was crying because I'd fallen off a pony, and said 'Never mind' to when I didn't have the nerve to be a jockey."

She smiled indulgently. "But since then you've learned to fight. And look at that last picture, when you were clinging to a ledge by one hand with a thousand-foot drop just below you—"

"Nerissa, dear Nerissa," I interrupted her. "I'll go to South Africa for you. I really will. But those fights in films—most of the time that isn't me; it's someone my size and shape who really does know judo. I don't. I can't fight at all. It's just my face in close-ups. And those ledges I was clinging to—certainly they were on a real rock face, but I was in no danger. I wouldn't have fallen a thousand feet, but only about ten, into one of those nets they use under trapeze acts in circuses. I did fall, two or three times. And there wasn't really a thousand feet below me —not sheer, anyway. We filmed it in the Valley of Rocks in North Devon, where there are a lot of little plateaus among the rock faces to stand the cameras on."

She listened with an air of being completely unconvinced. I reckoned it was useless to go on: to tell her that I was not a crack shot, couldn't fly an airplane or beat Olympic skiers downhill, couldn't speak Russian or build a radio transmitter or dismantle bombs, and would tell all at the first threat of torture. She knew different; she'd seen it with her own eyes. Her expression told me so.

"Well, all right," I said, capitulating. "I do know what should and should not go on in a racing stable. In England, anyway."

"And," she said complacently, "you can't say it wasn't you who did all that trick riding when you first went into films."

I couldn't. It was. But it had been nothing unique.

"I'll go and look at your horses, and see what your trainer says," I said; and thought that if he had no reasons to offer, I would be most unlikely to find any.

"Dear Edward, so kind . . ." She seemed suddenly weaker, as if the effort of persuading me had been too much. But when she saw the alarm on Charlie's face, and on mine, she raised a reassuring smile.

"Not yet, my dears. Another two months, perhaps . . . Two months at least, I think."

Charlie shook her head in protest, but Nerissa patted her hand. "It's all right, my dear. I've come to terms with it. But I want to arrange things . . . which is why I want Edward to see about the horses, and I really ought to explain . . ."

"Don't tire yourself," I said.

"I'm not . . . tired," she said, obviously untruthfully. "And I want to tell you. The horses used to belong to my sister, Portia, who married and went to live in South Africa thirty years ago. After she was widowed, she stayed there because all her friends were there, and I've been out to visit her several times over the years. I know I've told you about her."

We nodded.

"She died last winter," I said.

"Yes . . . a great sorrow." Nerissa looked a good deal more upset about her sister's death than about her own. "She had no close relatives except me, and she left me nearly everything she had inherited from her husband. And all her horses, too." She paused, as much to gather her forces as her thoughts. "They were yearlings. Expensive ones. And her trainer wrote to me to ask if I wanted to sell them, because we cannot bring South African horses to England owing to the African horse-sickness quarantine laws. But I thought it might be fun—interesting—to run them in South Africa, and then sell them for stud. But now—well, now I won't be here when they are old enough for stud, and meanwhile their value has dropped disastrously."

"Dearest Nerissa," Charlie said. "Does it matter?"

"Oh, yes. Yes, my dear, it does," she said positively. "Because I'm leaving them to my nephew, Danilo, and I don't like the idea of leaving him something worthless."

She looked from one of us to the other. "I can't remember—have you ever met Danilo?"

Charlie said, "No," and I said, "Once or twice, when he was a small boy. You used to bring him to the stables."

"That's right, so I did. And then of course my brother-in-law divorced that frightful woman, Danilo's mother, and took him to live in California with him. Well . . . Danilo has been back in England recently, and he has grown into such a nice young man. And isn't that lucky, my dears? Because, you see, I have so few relatives. In fact, really, Danilo is the only one, and even he is not a blood relative, his father being dear John's brother, do you see?"

We saw. John Cavesey, dead sixteen years or more, had been a country gent with four hunters and a sense of humor. He had also had Nerissa, no children, one brother, one nephew, and five square miles of Merrie England.

After a pause, Nerissa said, "I'll cable to Mr. Arknold—that's my trainer—to tell him you're coming to look into things, and to book some rooms for you."

"No, don't do that. He might resent your sending anyone, and I'd get no cooperation from him at all. I'll fix the rooms, and so on. And if you cable him, just say I might be calling in, out of interest, while I'm in South Africa on a short visit."

She smiled slowly and sweetly, and said, "You see, my dear, you do know how to investigate, after all."

3

I flew to Johannesburg five days later, equipped with a lot of facts and no faith in my ability to disentangle them.

Charlie and I had driven home from Nerissa's in a double state of depression. Poor Nerissa, we said. And poor us, losing her.

"And you've only just come home," Charlie added.

"Yes." I sighed. "Still . . . I couldn't have said no."

"No."

"Not that it'll do much good."

"You never know, you might spot something."

"Very doubtful."

"But," she said, with a touch of anxiety, "you will do your best?"

"Of course, love."

She shook her head. "You're cleverer than you think."

"Yeah," I said. "Sure."

She made a face, and we went some way in silence. Then she said, "When you went out to look at those two young chasers in her paddock, Nerissa told me what is the matter with her."

"Did she?"

Charlie nodded. "Some ghastly thing called Hodgkin's disease, which makes her glands swell, or something, and turn cellular, whatever that really means. She didn't know very clearly herself, I don't think. Except that it is absolutely fatal."

Poor Nerissa.

"She also told me," Charlie went on, "that she has left us a keepsake each in her will."

"Has she really?" I turned my head to look at Charlie. "How kind of her. Did she say what?"

"Keep your eyes on the road, for heaven's sake. No, she didn't say what. Just something to remember her by. She said she had quite enjoyed herself, drawing up her new will and giving people presents in it. Isn't she amazing?"

"She is."

"She really meant it. And she is so pleased that her nephew has turned out well. I've never seen anyone like that before—dying, and quite calm about it—and even enjoying things, like making a will—and knowing—knowing."

I glanced at her sidewise. Tears on Charlie's cheeks. She seldom cried, and didn't like to be watched.

I kept my eyes on the road.

I telephoned my agent and stunned him.

"B-But," he stuttered, "you never go anywhere, you always refuse. You thumped my table and shouted about it."

"Quite," I agreed. "But now I want a good reason for going to South Africa; so are any of my films due to open there soon, or are they not?"

"Well . . ." He sounded thoroughly disorganized. "Well, I'll have to look it up. And are you sure," he added in disbelief, "that if one of them is due to open, you really and truly want me to tell them you'll turn up in person?"

"That's what I said."

"Yes. I just don't believe it."

He rang back an hour later.

"There are two coming up. They are showing *One Way to Moscow* in Cape Town, starting Monday week. That's the first in a series of six revivals, so although *Moscow* itself is pretty old, you could turn up to give the whole lot a boost. Or there's the opening of *Rocks* in Johannesburg. But that's not until September 14th. Three weeks off. Is that soon enough?"

"Not really." I pondered. "It will have to be the Johannesburg one, though."

"All right. I'll fix it. And—er—does the sudden change of heart extend to chat shows and newspaper interviews?"

"No, it does not."

"I was afraid of that."

I had taken home from Nerissa's house all her trainer's letters, all the South African Racing Calendars, newspaper cuttings, and magazines she had been sent, and all the details of breeding and racing form of her eleven non-winning youngsters. A formidable bulk of paper, it had proved; and not miraculously easy to understand.

The picture which emerged, though, was enough to make anyone think, let alone the owner of the horses in question. Nine of the eleven had run nicely when they began their racing careers, and between December and May had clocked up a joint total of fourteen wins. Since the middle of May, none of them had finished nearer than fourth.

As far as I could judge from a limited squint at the leading-sires tables and the breeding-notes section of the South African *Horse and Hound*, all of them were of impeccable pedigree, and certainly, from the amounts she had paid out, Nerissa's sister Portia had bought no bargains. None of them had so far won enough prize money to cover their purchase price, and with every resounding defeat their future stud value, too, slid a notch toward zero.

As a bequest, the South African horses were a lump of lead.

Charlie came with me to Heathrow to see me off, as I had been home only nine days, which hadn't been long enough for either of us. While we were waiting at the check-in counter, half a dozen ladies asked for my autograph for their daughters, nephews, grandchildren, and a few eyes swiveled our way; and presently a dark-uniformed airline official appeared at our side and offered a small private room for waiting in. They were pretty good about that sort of thing, as I came through the airport fairly often, and we accepted gratefully.

"It's like being married to two people," Charlie said, with a sigh, sitting down. "The public you, and the private you. Quite separate. Do you know, if I see one of the films, or even a clip of one on the box, I look at the pictures of you, and I think, I slept with that man last night. And it seems extraordinary, because that public you doesn't really belong to me at all, but to all the people who pay to see you. And then you come home again, and you're just you, my familiar husband, and the public you is some other fellow."

I looked at her affectionately. "The private me has forgotten to pay the telephone bill."

"Well, damn it, I reminded you sixteen times."

"Will you pay it, then?"

"Well, I suppose so. But the telephone bill is one of your jobs. Checking all those cables, and those phone calls to America—I don't know what they should be. We're probably being overcharged if you don't check it."

"Have to risk it."

"Honestly!"

"It will be set off against tax, anyway."

"I suppose so."

I sat down beside her. The unpaid telephone bill was as good as anything else to talk about; we no longer needed to say aloud what we were saying to each other underneath. In all our life together, we had taken goodbyes casually, and hellos, too. A lot of people mistook it for not caring. It was perhaps too much the opposite. We needed each other like bees and honey.

When I landed at Jan Smuts International Airport sixteen hours later, I was met by a nervous man with damp palms who introduced himself as the South African Distribution Manager for Worldic Cinemas.

"Wenkins," he said. "Clifford Wenkins. So nice to see you."

He had restless eyes and a clipped South African accent. About forty. Never going to be successful. Talking a little too loudly, a little too familiarly, with the sort of uneasy bonhomie I found hardest to take.

As politely as possible, I removed my sleeve from his grasp.

"Nice of you to come," I said; and wished he hadn't.

"Couldn't let Edward Lincoln arrive without a reception, you know." He laughed loudly, out of nerves. I wondered idly why he should be so painfully self-conscious; as Distribution Manager he surely met film actors before breakfast every month of the year.

"Car over here." He walked crabwise in front of me, with his arms extended fore and aft, as if to push a path for me with the one and usher me along with the other. There were not enough people around for it to be remotely necessary.

I followed him, carrying my suitcase and making an effort to suffer his attentions gladly.

"Not far," he said anxiously, looking up placatingly at my face.

"Fine," I said.

There was a group of about ten people just inside the main doors. I looked at them in disillusion; their clothes and the way they stood had "media" stamped all over them, and it was without surprise that I saw the tape recorders and cameras sprout all over as soon as we drew near.

"Mr. Lincoln, what do you think of South Africa?"

"Hey, Link, how about a big smile?"

"Is there any truth in the rumor . . ."

"Our readers would like your views on . . ."

"Give us a smile."

I tried not to stop walking, but they slowed us down to a crawl. I smiled at them collectively and said soothing things like "I'm glad to be here. This is my first visit. I am looking forward to it very much," and eventually we persevered into the open air.

Clifford Wenkins's dampness extended to his brow, though the sunshine at six thousand feet above sea level was decidedly chilly.

"Sorry," he said, "but they would come."

"Marvelous how they knew the right day and the right time when my flight was only booked yesterday morning."

"Er . . . yes," he agreed weakly.

"I expect they are often willing to arrange publicity for people, when you want them to."

"Oh, yes, indeed," he agreed warmly.

I smiled at him. One could hardly blame him for using me as payment for past and future services, and I knew it was widely considered irrational that I preferred to avoid interviews. In many countries, the media gave you a rough passage if you wouldn't let them milk you for copy, and the South Africans had been more civil than most.

Wenkins rubbed his beaded forehead with one of the damp palms and said, "Let me take your suitcase."

I shook my head. "It isn't heavy," I said, and besides I was a good deal bigger than he was.

We walked across the car park to his car, and I experienced for the first time the extraordinary smell of Africa. A blend of hot sweet odors with a kink of mustiness: a strong disturbing smell which stayed in my nostrils for three or four days, until my scenting nerves got used to it and disregarded it. But my first overriding impression of South Africa was the way it smelled.

Smiling too much, sweating too much, talking too much, Clifford Wenkins drove me down the road to Johannesburg. The airport lay east of the city, out on the bare expanses of the Transvaal, and we were a good half hour reaching our destination.

"I hope everything will be all right for you," Wenkins said. "We don't often get—I mean, well—" He laughed jerkily. "Your agent was telling me on the telephone not to arrange any receptions or parties or radio shows or anything. I mean, we usually put on that sort of show for visiting stars—that is, er, of course, if Worldic are handling their films—but, er, we haven't done anything like that for you, and it seems all wrong to me. But then your agent insisted—and then your room—not in the city, he said. Not in the city itself, and not in a private house, he said, so I hope you will like—I mean, we were shattered—er, that is, honored—to hear you were coming."

Mr. Wenkins, I thought, you would get a lot further on in life if you didn't chatter so much. And aloud I said, "I'm sure everything will be fine."

"Yes, well . . . Er, if you don't want the usual round of things, though, what am I to arrange for you? I mean, there is a fortnight before the première of *Rocks,* don't you see? So what—?"

I didn't answer that one straight away. Instead I said, "This première. How much of a thing are you making of it?"

"Oh." He laughed again at nothing funny. "Er, well, big, of course. Invitations. Tickets in aid of charity. All the glitter, old boy—er, I mean—sorry—er, well, Worldic said to push the boat right out, you see, once they'd got over the shock, that is."

"I do see." I sighed slightly. I had chosen to do the damn thing, I thought. So I ought, in all fairness, to give them value for their trouble.

"Look," I said, "if you want to, and if you think anyone would want to come, go ahead and arrange some sort of drinks-and-canapés affair either before or after the showing of the film, and I'll go to that. And one morning soon, if you'd like to, you could ask all those good friends of yours at the airport, and any others in their trade that you want to include, to meet us somewhere for coffee or a drink or something. How would that do?"

He was dumb with surprise. I looked across at him. His mouth was opening and shutting like a fish.

I laughed to myself. Nerissa had a lot to answer for.

"The rest of the time, don't worry about me. I'll amuse myself all right. For one thing, I'll go to the races."

"Oh." He finally overcame the jaw problem and got the two halves into proper working order. "Er—I could get someone to take you there, if you like."

"We'll see," I said noncommittally.

The journey ended at the Iguana Rock, a very pleasant country hotel on the northern edge of the city. The management gave me a civil greeting and a luxurious room and indicated that a clap of the hands would bring anything from iced water to dancing girls, as required.

"I would like to hire a car," I said, and Wenkins gushed forth to say it was all arranged, he had arranged it; a chauffeur-driven pumpkin would be constantly on call, courtesy of Worldic.

I shook my head. "Courtesy of me," I said. "Didn't my agent tell you that I intended to pay all the expenses of my trip myself?"

"Well, he did, yes, but Worldic say they'd like to pick up the tab."

"No," I said.

He laughed nervously. "No. . . . Well, I see, er, I mean—yes." He spluttered to a stop. The eyes darted around restlessly, the hands gestured vaguely, the meaningless smile twitched his mouth convulsively, and he couldn't stand still on his two feet. I didn't usually throw people into such a tizzy, and I wondered what on earth my agent could have said to him to bring him to such a state.

He managed eventually to get himself out of the Iguana and back to his car, and his departure was a great relief. Within an hour, however, he was on the telephone.

"Would tomorrow, er, morning—suit you for, er, I mean, the press?"

"Yes," I said.

"Then, er, would you ask your driver to take you to, er, Randfontein House, er—the Dettrick Room? That's a reception room, you see, which we hire for this, well, sort of thing."

"What time?"

"Oh . . . say eleven-thirty. Could you—er—get there at about eleven-thirty?"

"Yes," I said briefly again, and after a few further squirms he said he would look forward—er—to seeing me then.

I put the receiver down, finished unpacking, drank some coffee, summoned up the pumpkin, and went briskly off to the races.

4

Flat racing in South Africa took place on Wednesdays and Saturdays throughout the year, but only occasionally on other days. Accordingly, it had seemed good sense to arrive in Johannesburg on Wednesday morning and to go to the only race meeting in South Africa that day, at Newmarket.

I paid to go in, and bought a race card. One of Nerissa's constant failures, I saw, was due to have another go later in the afternoon.

Newmarket was Newmarket the world over. Stands, crowds, horses, bookmakers; atmosphere of bustle and purpose; air of tradition and order. All were much the same. I wandered across to the parade ring, where the runners for the first race were already walking round. Same little clumps of owners and trainers standing in hopeful conversations in the middle. Same earnest racegoers leaning on the rails and studying the wares.

Differences were small. The horses, to English eyes, looked slightly smaller-framed and had very upright fetlocks, and they were led round, not by white stable lads in their own darkish clothes, but by black stableboys in long white coats.

On the principle of backing only horses I knew something about, I kept my hands in my pockets. The jockeys in their bright silks came out and mounted; the runners went away down the track and scurried back, hoofs rattling on the bone-dry ground. I strolled down from the stands to search for and identify Nerissa's trainer, Greville Arknold. He had a runner in the following race, and somewhere he would be found saddling it up.

In the event, I hardly had to look. On my way to the saddling boxes, a young man touched me on the arm.

"I say," he said, "aren't you Edward Lincoln?"

I nodded and half smiled, and kept on walking.

"Guess I'd better introduce myself. Danilo Cavesey. I believe you know my aunt."

That stopped me, all right. I put out my hand, and he shook it warmly.

"I heard you were coming, of course. Aunt Nerissa cabled Greville you were on your way out here for some film première, and would he look out for you at the races. So I was kind of expecting you, you see."

His accent was a slow Californian drawl full of lazy warmth. It was instantly clear why Nerissa had liked him. His sun-tanned good-looking face, his open, pleasant expression, his clean, casual, blond-brown hair—all were in the best tradition of American youth.

"She didn't say you were in South Africa," I commented, surprised.

"Well, no." He wrinkled his nose disarmingly. "I don't believe she knows. I only flew out here a few days ago, on a vacation. Say, how is the old girl? She wasn't all that sprightly when I last visited with her."

He was smiling happily. He didn't know.

I said, "She's pretty ill, I'm afraid."

"Is that so? I'm sure sorry to hear that. I must write her, tell her I'm out here, tell her I'm taking a look-see into the state of the horses."

"The state of the horses?" I echoed.

"Oh, sure. Aunt Nerissa's horses out here are not running good. Stinking bad, to be accurate." He grinned cheerfully. "I shouldn't bet on number eight in the fourth race, if you want to die rich."

"Thanks," I said. "She did mention to me that they were not doing so well just now."

"I'll bet she did. They wouldn't win if you gave them a ten-minute start and nobbled the others."

"Is there any reason for it, do you know?"

"Search me." He shrugged. "Greville's real chewed up about it. Says he hasn't had anything like this happen before."

"Not a virus?" I suggested.

"Can't be. Otherwise all the others would get it, too, not just Aunt Nerissa's. We've been talking it over, you see. Greville just hasn't an idea."

"I'd like to meet him," I said casually.

"Oh, sure. Yes, indeed. But say, why don't we get out of this wind and have ourselves a beer or something? Greville has this starter right now, but he'll be happy to see us later on."

"All right," I said, and we went and had ourselves the beer. Danilo was right: the south wind was cold and spring was still a hint and a memory.

Danilo, I judged, was about twenty years old. He had bright blue eyes and blond-brown eyelashes, and his teeth were California-straight. He had the untouched air of one to whom the rigors of life had not yet happened; a boy not necessarily spoiled, but one to whom much had been given.

He was at the University of California at Berkeley studying political science, he said, with one more year to do. "This time next summer, I'll be all through with college."

"What do you plan to do after that?" I asked, making conversation.

There was a flash of amusement in the blue eyes. "Oh, I guess I'll have to think of something, but I've nothing lined up right now."

The future could take care of itself, I thought, and reflected that for golden boys like Danilo it usually did.

We watched the next race together. Greville's starter finished third, close up.

"Too bad," Danilo sighed. "I just had it on the nose, not across the boards."

"Did you lose much?" I asked sympathetically.

"I guess not. Just a few rand."

Rands came just under two to the pound sterling, or about one to $1.40. He couldn't have done himself much harm.

We walked down from the stands and over toward the unsaddling enclosures. "Do you know something?" he said. "You're not a bit what I expected."

"In what way?" I asked, smiling.

"Oh, I guess . . . For a big movie star, I expected some sort of, well, *presence*. You know?"

"Off the screen, movie actors are as dim as anyone else."

He glanced at me suspiciously, but I wasn't laughing at him. I meant it. He had a much more naturally luminous personality than I had. I might have been an inch or two taller, an inch or two broader across the shoulders, but the plus factor had nothing to do with size.

The man stalking round the horse which had finished third, peering judiciously at its legs and running a probing hand along its loin, was a burly thickset man with an air of dissatisfaction.

"That's Greville." Danilo nodded, following my gaze.

The trainer spoke briefly to a woman Danilo identified to me as the horse's owner. His manner, from twenty feet away, looked brusque and far from conciliatory. I knew trainers had to grow hard skins if they were to stay sane: one could not forever be apologizing to owners if their horses got beaten; one had to make them realize that regardless of the oats and exercise crammed into them, maybe other people's horses could actually run faster. But Greville Arnold appeared plainly disagreeable.

After a while, the horses were led away and the crowd

thinned out. Arknold listened, with a pinched mouth and a stubborn backward tilt of the head, to what looked almost like apologies from the woman owner. She came to a stop, got no melting response from him, shrugged, turned slowly, and walked away.

Arknold's gaze rose from down his nose and fastened on Danilo. He stared for a moment, then raised his eyebrows questioningly. Danilo very slightly jerked his head in my direction, and Arknold transferred his attention to me.

Again the slow appraisal. Then he came across.

Danilo introduced us with an air of what fun it was for us to know each other. A mutual privilege.

Great.

I didn't take to Greville Arknold, either then or over after. Yet he was pleasant enough to me: smiled, shook hands, said he was glad to meet me, said that Mrs. Cavesey had cabled to say I might be coming to the races, and to look after me if I did.

He had a perceptible Afrikaans accent, and like many South Africans he was, I discovered later, trilingual in English, Afrikaans, and Zulu. He had a face formed of thick slabs of flesh, lips so thin that they hardly existed, the scars of old acne over his chin and down his neck, and a bristly ginger mustache one inch by two below his nose. And for all the smiling and the welcoming chat, he had cold eyes.

"Your horse ran well just then," I suggested conversationally.

The recent anger reappeared at once in his manner. "That stupid woman insisted that her horse run today when I wanted to run it Saturday instead. He had a hard race at Turffontein last Saturday. He needed another three days' rest."

"She looked as if she were apologizing," I said.

"Yes. She was. Too late, of course. She should have had more sense. Decent colt, that. Would have won on Saturday. No sense. Owners always ought to do what a trainer says. They pay for expert knowledge, don't they? So they always ought to do what the expert says."

I smiled vaguely, noncommittally. As an owner myself, even of only one moderate steeplechasing gelding, I disagreed with him about always. Sometimes, even usually, yes. But always, no. I knew of at least one Grand National winner which would never have gone to the start if the owner had paid attention to the trainer's advice.

"I see Mrs. Cavesey has a runner in the fourth," I said.

The dogmatic look faded to be replaced by a slight frown.

"Yes," Arknold said. "I expect she may have mentioned to you that her horses are not doing well."

"She told me you had no idea why," I said, nodding.

He shook his head. "I cannot understand it. They get the same treatment as all the others. Same food, same exercise, everything. They are not ill. I have had a veterinarian examine them, several times. It is worrying. Very."

"It must be," I said sympathetically.

"And dope tests!" he said. "We must have had a hundred dope tests. All negative, the whole lot."

"Do they look fit?" I asked. "I mean, would you expect them to do better, from the way they look?"

"See for yourself." He shrugged. "That is . . . I don't know how much of a judge of horses you are."

"Bound to be a pretty good one, I'd say," said Danilo positively. "After all, it's no secret his old man was a stable hand."

"Is that so?" he said. "Then perhaps you would like to see round the stables? Maybe you could even come up with some suggestion about Mrs. Cavesey's string; you never know."

The irony in his voice made it clear that he thought that impossible. Which meant that either he really did not know what was the matter with the horses or he did know but was absolutely certain that I would not find out.

"I'd like very much to see the stables," I said.

"Good. Then you shall. How about tomorrow evening? Walk round with me, at evening stables. Four-thirty."

I nodded.

"That's fixed, then. And you, Danilo. Do you want to come as well?"

"That would be just fine, Greville. I sure would."

So it was settled; and Danilo said he would come and pick me up at the Iguana Rock himself.

Chink, Nerissa's runner in the fourth race, looked good enough in the parade ring, with a healthy bloom on his coat and muscles seeming strong, free, and loose. There wasn't a great deal of substance about him, but he had an intelligent head and strong, well-placed shoulders. Nerissa's sister, Portia, had given twenty-five thousand rand for him as a yearling on the strength of his breeding, and he had won only one race, his first, way back in April.

"What do you think of him, Link?" Danilo asked, leaning his hip against the parade-ring rail.

"He looks fit enough," I said.

"Yeah. They all do, Greville says."

Chink was being led round by two stable lads, one each side. Nothing wrong with Arknold's security arrangements.

Because of the upright fetlocks, I found it hard to judge the degree of spring in Chink's stride. All the horses looked to me as if they were standing on their toes, a condition I imagined was caused by living from birth on hard dry ground. Certainly he went down to the post moving no more scratchily than the others, and he lined up in the stalls and bounded out of them with no trouble. I watched every step of his journey through my Zeiss eight-by-fifties.

He took the first half mile without apparent effort, lying about sixth, nice and handy, just behind the leading bunch. When they turned in to the straight for home, the leaders quickened, but Chink didn't. I saw the head of the jockey bob and the rest of his body become energetically busy trying to keep the horse going; but when a jockey has to work like that on a horse a long way out, he might as well not bother. Chink had run out of steam, and the best rider in the world could have done nothing about that.

I put down my race glasses. The winner fought a ding-dong, the crowd roared, and Chink returned unsung, unbacked, unwatched, and a good thirty lengths later.

With Danilo, I went down to where he was being unsaddled, and joined Greville Arknold in his aura of perplexed gloom.

"There you are," he said. "You saw for yourself."

"I did," I said.

Chink was sweating and looked tired. He stood still, with drooping head, as if he felt the disgrace.

"What do you think?" Arknold asked.

I shook my head. He had in fact looked plainly like a slow horse, yet on his breeding, and the fast time of the race he had won, he should not be.

He and the other ten could not all have bad hearts, or bad teeth, or blood disorders, all undetected. Not after those thorough veterinary investigations. And not *all* of them. It was impossible.

They had not all been ridden every time by the same jockey. There were, I discovered from Nerissa's racing papers, very few jockeys in South Africa compared with England: only thirteen jockeys and twenty-two apprentices riding on the Natal tracks near Durban, the supposed center of the sport.

There were four main racing areas; the Johannesburg tracks in the Transvaal, the Pietermaritzburg-Durban tracks in Natal, the Port Elizabeth tracks in the Eastern Cape, and the Cape Town tracks in Cape Province. Various ones of Nerissa's horses had been to all four areas, had been ridden by the local bunch of jockeys, and had turned in the same results.

Fast until May, dead slow from June onward.

The fact that they moved around meant that it probably could not be attributed to something in their base quarters.

No illness. No dope. No fixed address. No common jockey.

All of which pointed to one solution. One source of disaster.

The trainer himself.

It was easy enough for a trainer to make sure a horse of his didn't win, if he had a mind to. He merely had to give it too severe an exercise gallop too soon before a race. Enough races had, in sober fact, been lost that way by accident for it to be impossible to prove that anyone had done it on purpose.

Trainers seldom nobbled their own horses, because they had demonstrably more to gain if they won. But it looked to me as if it had to be Arknold who was responsible, even if the method he was using turned out to be the simplest in the world.

I thought the solution to Nerissa's problem lay in transferring her string to a different trainer.

I thought I might just as well go straight home and tell her so.

Two nasty snags.

I was committed to a première two weeks off.

And I might guess who and how, about the horses.

But I had no idea *why*.

5

The ladies and gentlemen of the press (or, in other words, a partially shaven, polo-neck sweatered, elaborately casual, and uninformed mob) yawned to their feet when I reached the Dettrick Room in Randfontein House within ticking distance of half past eleven.

Clifford Wenkins had met me in the hall, twittering as before, and with wetter than ever palms. We rode up in the lift together, with him explaining to me exactly whom he had asked, and who had come. Interviewers from two radio programs. He hoped I wouldn't mind? They would be happy just to tape my answers to their questions. Just into a microphone. If I didn't mind? And then there were the dailies, the weeklies, the ladies' magazines, and one or two people who had flown up especially from Cape Town and Durban.

I wished I hadn't suggested it. Too late to run away.

The only thing to do, I thought as the lift hissed to a halt and the doors slid open, was to put on a sort of performance. To act.

"Wait a minute," I said to Wenkins.

He stopped with me outside the lift as the doors shut again behind us.

"What is it?" he asked anxiously.

"Nothing. I just need a few seconds before we go in."

He didn't understand, though what I was doing was not a process by any means confined to professional actors. Girding up the loins, the Bible called it. Getting the adrenaline on the move. Making the heart beat faster. Shifting the mental gears into top. Politicians could do it in three seconds flat.

"O.K.," I said.

He sighed with relief, walked across the hallway, and opened a heavy polished door opposite.

We went in.

They unfolded themselves from sofas and carpet, pushed themselves tiredly off the walls, stubbed out one or two cigarettes, and went on puffing at others.

"Hi," said one of the men, and the others, like a sort of jungle pack, watched and waited. He was one of those who had been at the airport. He had no reason, as none of them had, to believe I would now be any different.

"Hullo," I said.

Well, I could always do it if I really wanted to. Almost every well-trained actor can.

I watched them loosen, saw the tiredness go out of their manner and the smile creep into their eyes. They wouldn't chew me to bits in their columns now, even if they still came across with those carefully sharpened questions they all had ready in their notebooks.

The man who had said hi, their apparently natural leader, put out his hand to be shaken and said, "I'm Roderick Hodge of the Rand *Daily Star*. Features Editor."

Late thirties, but trying to ignore the passage of time: young haircut, young clothes, young affectation of speech. A certain panache about him, but also some of the ruthless cynicism of experienced journalists.

I shook his hand and smiled at him as a friend. I needed him to be one.

"Look," I said, "unless you are all in a hurry, why

don't we sit down again, and then you can all ask whatever you like, perhaps in groups, and maybe I can move around a bit; and then everyone might have more time for things than if I just sort of stand here in front of you."

They thought that was all right. No one was in much of a hurry, they said. Roderick said dryly that no one would go before the booze started flowing, and the atmosphere started mellowing nicely into an all-pals-together trade meeting.

They mostly asked the personal questions first.

According to their calculations, I was thirty-three. Was that right?

It was.

And married? Yes. Happily? Yes. My first or second marriage? First. And her first? Yes.

They wanted to know how many children I had, with their names and ages. They asked how many rooms my house had, and what it had cost. How many cars, dogs, horses, yachts I had. How much I earned in a year, how much I had been paid for *Rocks*.

How much did I give my wife to buy clothes with? Did I think a woman's place was in the home?

"In the heart," I said flippantly, which pleased the women's-mag girl who had asked, but was slightly sick-making to all the others.

Why didn't I go to live in a tax haven? I liked England. An expensive luxury? Very. And was I a millionaire? Perhaps some days, on paper, when share prices went up. If I was as rich as that, why did I work? To pay taxes, I said.

Clifford Wenkins had summoned up some caterers, who brought coffee and cheese biscuits and bottles of Scotch. The press poured the whiskey into the coffee and sighed contentedly. I kept mine separate, but had great difficulty in explaining to the waiter that I did not like my liquor diluted in nine times as much water. In South Africa, I had already discovered, they tended to fill up the tumblers; and I supposed it made sense as a long drink in a hot climate, but while it was so cold it merely ruined good Scotch.

Clifford Wenkins eyed my small drink in its large glass.
"Let me get you some water."

"I've got some. I prefer it like this."

"Oh . . . really?"

He scuttled busily away and came back with an earnestly bearded man trailing a hand microphone and a long
lead. There was no sense of humor behind the beard,
which made, I thought, for a fairly stodgy interview, but
he assured me afterward that what I had said was just
right, just perfect for a five-minute slot in his Saturday
evening show. He took back the microphone which I had
been holding, shook me earnestly by the hand, and disappeared into a large array of recording equipment in one
corner.

After that I was supposed to do a second interview, this
time for a women's program, but some technical hitches
had developed in the gear.

I moved, in time, right round the room, sitting on the
floor, on the arms of chairs, leaning on the window sills,
or just plain standing.

Loosened by the Scotch, they asked the other questions.

What did I think of South Africa? I liked it.

What were my opinions of their political scene? I
hadn't any, I said. I had been in their country only one
day. One couldn't form opinions in that time.

Most people arrived with them already formed, they
observed. I said I didn't think that was sensible.

Well, what were my views on racial discrimination? I
said without heat that I thought any form of discrimination was bound to give rise to some injustice. I said I
thought it a pity that various people found it necessary to
discriminate against women, Jews, aborigines, American
Indians, and a friend of mine in Nairobi who couldn't get
promotion in a job he excelled at because he was white.

I also said I couldn't answer any more of that sort of
question, and could we please get off politics and civil
rights, unless they would like me to explain the differences
between the economic theories of the Tory and the Labour
parties.

They laughed. No, they said. They wouldn't.

They reverted to films and asked questions I felt better able to answer.

Was it true I had started as a stunt man? Sort of, I said. I rode horses across everything from Robin Hood via Bosworth Field to the Charge of the Light Brigade. Until one day, when I was doing a bit of solo stuff, a director called me over, gave me some words to say, and told me I was in. Good clean romantic stuff, for which I apologized. It did happen sometimes like that, though.

And then? Oh, then I got given a better part in his next film. And how old was I at the time? Twenty-two, just married, living on baked beans in a basement flat in Hammersmith, and still attending part-time speech and drama classes, as I had for three years.

I was standing more or less in the center of the room when the door opened behind me. Clifford Wenkins turned his head to see who it was, frowned with puzzlement, and went busily across to deal with the situation.

"I'm afraid you can't come in here," he was saying. "This is a private room. Private reception. I'm sorry, but would you mind—I say, you can't . . . this is a private room. I say—"

I gathered Wenkins was losing. Not surprising, really.

Then I felt the clump on the shoulder and heard the familiar fruity voice.

"Link, dear boy. Do tell this—er—person that we are old buddy buddies. He doesn't seem to want me to come in. Now, I ask you."

I turned round. Stared in surprise. Said to Wenkins, "Perhaps you would let him stay. I do know him. He's a cameraman."

Conrad raised his eyebrows sharply. "Director of Photography, dear boy. A cameraman indeed!"

"Sorry," I said ironically. "Have a Scotch?"

"Now, that, dear boy, is more like it."

Wenkins gave up the struggle and went off to get Conrad a drink. Conrad surveyed the relaxed atmosphere, the hovering smoke, the empty cups and half-empty glasses, and the gentle communicators chatting in seated groups.

"My God," he said. "My great God. I don't believe it. I didn't, in fact, believe it when they told me Edward Lincoln was giving a press conference right here in Johannesburg at this very moment. I bet on it not being true. So they told me where. In that ritzy room at the top of the Randfontein, they said. Go and see for yourself. So I did."

A laugh began rumbling somewhere down in his belly and erupted in a coughing guffaw.

"Shut up," I said.

He spread his arms wide, embracing the room. "They don't know, they just don't know what they're seeing, do they? They've just no idea."

"Be quiet, Conrad, damn it," I said.

He went on wheezing away in uncontainable chuckles. "My dear boy. I didn't know you could do it. Off the set, that is. Talk about a lot of tame tigers eating out of your hand. . . . Just wait until Evan hears."

"He isn't likely to," I said comfortably. "Not from five thousand or so miles away."

He shook with amusement. "Oh, no, dear boy. He's right here in Johannesburg. Practically in the next street."

"He can't be!"

"We've been here since Sunday." He choked off the last of his laughter and wiped his eyes with his thumb. "Come and have some lunch, dear boy, and I'll tell you all about it."

I looked at my watch. Twelve-twenty.

"In a while, then. I've still got one more bit of taping to do, when they get hold of a spare microphone."

Roderick Hodge detached himself from a group by one of the windows and brought a decorative female over with him, and Clifford Wenkins dead-heated with Conrad's drink.

The girl, the would-be interviewer from the women's radio program, had the sort of face that would have been plain on a different personality; but she also had a bushy mop of curly brown hair, enormous yellow rimmed sunglasses, and a sticklike figure clad in an orange-and-tan checked trouser suit. The spontaneous friendliness in her manner saved her from any impression of caricature. Conrad took in her color temperature with an appreciative eye while explaining he had been engaged on four films with me in the recent past.

Roderick's attention sharpened like an adjusted focus.

"What is he like to work with?" he demanded.

"That's not fair," I said.

Neither Roderick nor Conrad paid any attention. Conrad looked at me judiciously, pursed his lips, lifted up a hand, and bent the fingers over one by one as he rolled his tongue lovingly around the words.

"Patient, powerful, punctual, professional, and puritanical." And aside to me he stage-whispered, "How's that?"

"Ham," I said.

Roderick predictably pounced on the last one. "Puritanical. How do you mean?"

Conrad was enjoying himself. "All his leading ladies complain that he kisses them with art, not heart."

I could see the headlines writing themselves in Roderick's head. His eye was bright.

"My sons don't like it," I said.

"What?"

"When the elder one saw me in a film kissing someone who wasn't his mother, he wouldn't speak to me for a week."

They laughed.

But at the time it had been far from funny. Peter had also started wetting his bed again at five years old and had cried a lot, and a child psychiatrist had told us it was because he felt insecure: he felt his foundations were slipping away, because Daddy kissed other ladies, and quarreled with Mummy at home. It had happened so soon after Libby's accident that we wondered whether he was also worrying about that; but we had never told him Libby had been ill because he had dropped her, and never intended to. One couldn't burden a child with that sort of knowledge, because a pointless, unnecessary feeling of guilt could have distorted the whole of his development.

"What did you do about that?" the girl asked sympathetically.

"Took him to some good clean horror films instead."

"Oh, yeah," Conrad said.

Clifford Wenkins came twittering back from another of his darting foraging expeditions. Sweat still lay in pearl-sized beads in the furrows of his forehead. How did he cope, I vaguely wondered, when summer came?

He thrust a stick microphone triumphantly into my hands. Its lead ran back to the corner where the radio apparatus stood. "There we are—er—all fixed, I mean." He looked in unnecessary confusion from me to the girl. "There we are, Katya, dear. Er—all ready, I think."

I looked at Conrad. I said, "I learned just one word of Afrikaans at the races yesterday, and you can do it while I tape this interview."

Conrad said suspiciously, "What word?"

"*Voetsek*," I said conversationally.

They all split themselves politely. *Voetsek* meant bugger off.

Conrad's chuckles broke out again like a recurring infection when they explained.

"If only Evan could see this," he said, wheezing.

"Let's forget Evan," I suggested.

Conrad put his hand on Roderick's arm and took him away, each of them enjoying a separate joke.

Katya's smallish eyes were laughing behind the enormous yellow specs. "And to think they said that at the airport you were the chilliest of cold fish."

I gave her a sidewise smile. "Maybe I was tired." I eyed the notebook she clutched in one hand. "What sort of things are you going to ask?"

"Oh, only the same as the others, I should think." But there was a mischievous glint of teeth that boded no good.

"All set, Katya," a man called from the row of electronic boxes and dials. "Any time you say."

"Right." She looked down at the notebook and then up at me. I was about three feet away from her, holding my glass in one hand and the microphone in the other. She considered this with her curly head on one side, then took a large step closer. Almost touching.

"That's better, I think. There will be too much background noise if either of us is too far from that microphone. It's an old one, by the looks of it. Oh, and maybe I'd better hold it. You look a bit awkward." She took the microphone and called across the room. "O.K., Joe, switch on."

Joe switched on.

Katya jerked appallingly from head to foot, arched backward through the air, and fell to the floor.

The murmuring peaceful faces turned, gasped, cried out, screwed themselves up in horror.

"Switch off!" I shouted urgently. "Switch everything off. At once!"

Roderick took two strides and bent over Katya with outstretched hands to help her, and I pulled him back.

"Get Joe to switch that bloody microphone off first, or you will take the shock as well."

The Joe in question ran over, looking ill.

"I have," he said. "It's off now."

I thought that all, that any of them would know what to do, and do it. But they just stood and knelt around looking at me, as if it were up to me to know, to do, to be the resourceful man in all those films who always took the lead, always.

Oh, God, I thought. Just look at them. And there was no time to waste. No time at all. She was no longer breathing.

I knelt down beside her and took her glasses off. Pulled open the neck of her shirt. Stretched her head back. Put my mouth on hers, and blew my breath into her lungs.

"Get a doctor," Roderick said. "And an ambulance. Oh, Christ . . . Hurry. Hurry!"

I breathed into her. Not too hard. Just with the force of

breath. But over and over, heaving her chest up and down.

A lethal electric voltage stops the heart.

I tried to feel a pulse beating in her neck, but couldn't find one. Roderick understood what I was doing and picked up her wrist, but it was no good there either. His face was agonized. Katya was a great deal more, it seemed, than just a colleague.

Two thousand years passed like two more minutes. Roderick put his ear down on Katya's left breast. I went on breathing air into her, feeling as the seconds passed that it was no good, that she was dead. Her flesh was the color of death, and very cold.

He heard the first thud before I felt it. I saw it in his face. Then there were two separate jolts in the blood vessel I had my fingers on under her jaw, and then some uneven, jerky little bumps, and then at last, unbelievably, slow, rhythmic, and strengthening, the life-giving ba-boom ba-boom ba-boom of a heart back in business.

Roderick's mouth tightened and twisted as he raised his head, and the cords in his neck stood out with the effort he was putting into not weeping. But the tears of relief ran down his cheeks for all that, and he tried to get rid of them with his fingers.

I pretended not to see, if that was what he wanted. But I knew, heaven forgive me, that one day I would put that face, that reaction, into a film. Whatever one learned, whatever one saw, and however private it was, in the end, if one was an actor, one used it.

She breathed in convulsively on her own while I was still breathing in myself, through my nose. It felt extraordinary, as if she were sucking the air out of me.

I took my mouth away from hers, and stopped holding her jaws open with my hands. She went on breathing, a bit sketchily at first, but then quite regularly, in shallow, body-shaking, audible gasps.

"She ought to be warmer," I said to Roderick. "She needs blankets."

He looked at me dazedly. "Yes. Blankets."

"I'll get some," someone said, and the breath-held quietness in the room erupted with sudden bustle. Frozen shock turned to worried shock, and that to relieved shock, and from that to revival via the whiskey bottle.

I saw Clifford Wenkins looking down at Katya's still unconscious form. His face was gray and looked like putty oozing; the sweat had not had time to dry. For once, however, he had been reduced to speechlessness.

Conrad, too, seemed temporarily to have run out of "dear boy"s. But I guessed sharply that the blankness in his face as he watched the proceedings was not the result of shock. He was at his business, as I had been at mine, seeing an electrocution in terms of camera angles, atmospheric shadows, impact-making colors. And at what point, I wondered, did making use of other people's agonies become a spiritual sin?

Someone reappeared with some blankets, and with shaking hands Roderick wrapped Katya up in them, and put a cushion under her head.

I said to him, "Don't expect too much when she wakes up. She'll be confused, I think."

He nodded. Color was coming back to her cheeks. She seemed securely alive. The time of fiercest anxiety was over.

He looked suddenly up at me, then down at her, then up at me again. The first thought that was not raw emotion was taking root.

As if it were a sudden discovery, he slowly said, "You're Edward Lincoln."

For him, too, the dilemma of conscience arose: whether or not to make professional copy out of the near death of his girl friend.

I looked round the room, and so did he. There had been a noticeable thinning of the ranks. I met Roderick's eyes and knew what he was thinking; the press had made for the telephones, and he was the only one there from the Rand *Daily Star*.

He looked down again at the girl. "She'll be all right now, won't she?" he said.

I made an inconclusive gesture with my hands and didn't directly answer. I didn't know whether or not she would be all right. I thought her heart had probably not been stopped for much over three minutes, so with a bit of luck her brain would not be irreparably damaged. But my knowledge was only the sketchy remains of a long-past first-aid course.

The journalist in Roderick won the day. He stood up abruptly and said, "Do me a favor? Don't let them take her to hospital or anywhere before I get back."

"I'll do my best," I said; and he made a highly rapid exit.

Joe, the radio equipment man, was coiling up the lead of the faulty microphone, having disconnected it gingerly from its power socket. He looked at it dubiously and said, "It's such an old one I didn't know we had it. It was just there, in the box. . . . I wish to God I hadn't decided to use it. It just seemed quicker than waiting any longer for the replacement from the studio. I'll make sure it'll do no more damage, anyway. I'll dismantle it and throw it away."

Conrad returned to my side and stood looking down at Katya, who began showing signs of returning consciousness. Her eyelids fluttered. She moved under the blankets.

Conrad said, "You do realize, dear boy, that until very shortly before the accident you were holding that microphone yourself."

"Yes," I said neutrally. "I do."

"And," said Conrad, "just how many people in this room showed the slightest sign of knowing that the only hope for the electrocuted is artificial respiration, instantly applied?"

I looked at him straightly.

"Did you know?"

He sighed. "You are so cynical, dear boy. But, no, I didn't."

6

Danilo arrived at the Iguana Rock at four o'clock with a hired Triumph, a scarlet open-necked shirt, and a sun-tanned grin.

I had been back there less than an hour myself, Conrad and I having dawdled over a beer-and-sandwich lunch in an unobtrusive bar. Katya had gone to hospital, with Roderick in frantic tow, and the other journalists were currently stubbing their fingernails on their typewriters. Clifford Wenkins had twittered off at some unmarked point in the proceedings, and when Conrad and I left we saw him, too, engaged in earnest conversation on the telephone. Reporting to Worldic, no doubt. I stifled a despairing sigh. Not a butterfly's chance in a blizzard that anyone would ignore the whole thing as uninteresting.

Danilo chatted in his carefree way, navigating us round the elevated Sir de Villiers Graaf ring road, God's gift to the city's inhabitants which took the through traffic out of their way, over their heads.

"I can't imagine what Johannesburg was like before they built this highway," Danilo commented. "They still have a big traffic problem downtown, and as for parking—there's more cars parked along the streets down there than one-armed bandits in Nevada."

"You've been here quite a time, then?"

"Hell, no," he said, grinning. "Only a few days. But I've been here before, once, and anyway it only takes twenty minutes of searching around to teach you that all the car parks are permanently full and that you can never park within a quarter-mile of where you want to be."

He drove expertly and coolly on what was to him the wrong side of the road.

"Greville lives down near Turffontein," he said. "We drop down off this elevated part soon now. . . . Did that sign say Eloff Street Extension?"

"It did," I confirmed.

"Great." He took the turn and we left the South African M. 1. and presently passed some football fields and a skating rink.

"They call this Wembley," Danilo said. "And over there is a lake called Wemmer Pan, for boating. And, say, they have a water organ there which shoots colored fountains up into the air in time to the music."

"Have you been there?"

"No . . . Greville told me, I guess. He also says it's a great place for fishing out rotting corpses and headless torsos."

"Nice," I said.

He grinned.

Before we reached Turffontein, he turned off down a side road which presently became hard impacted earth covered with a layer of dust.

"They've had no rain here for four or five months," Danilo said. "Everything's sure looking dry."

The grass was certainly brownish, but that was what I expected. I was surprised to learn from Danilo that in a month's time, when the rain came and the days were warmer, the whole area would be lush, colorful, and green.

"It's too bad you won't be here to see the jacarandas," Danilo said. "They'll flower all over, after you've gone."

"You've seen them before?"

He hesitated. "Well, no, not exactly. Last time I was here, they weren't flowering. It's just what Greville says."

"I see," I said.

"Here it is. This is Greville's place, right in here." He pointed, then turned in between some severe-looking brick pillars, and drove up a gravel drive into a stable which looked as if it had been transplanted straight from England.

Arknold himself was already out in the yard talking to a black African whom he introduced as his head boy, Barty. Arknold's head lad looked as tough as himself: a solid strong-looking man of about thirty, with a short thick neck and unsmiling cold eyes. He was the first black African I had seen, I thought in mild surprise, whose natural expression had not been good-natured.

There was nothing in his manner, however, but civility, and he nodded to Danilo's greeting with the ordinary acknowledgment of people who meet each other fairly often.

Arknold said that everything was ready, and we started looking round the boxes without more ado. The horses were all like those I had seen on the track: up on their toes, with slightly less bone all round than those at home.

There was nothing at all to distinguish Nerissa's horses from their stablemates. They looked as well, had legs as firm, eyes as bright; and they were not all stabled in one block, but were scattered among the rest. Colts in one quadrangle, fillies in another. Everything as it should be, as it normally would be in England.

The lads—the boys—were all young and all black. Like lads the world over, they were possessively proud of the horses they cared for, though alongside this pride there emerged a second, quite definite pattern of behavior.

They responded to me with smiles, to Arknold with respect, and to Barty with unmistakable fear.

I had no knowledge of what sort of tribal hold he had over them, and I never did find out, but in their wary eyes and their shrinking away at his approach, one could see he held them in a bondage far more severe than any British head lad could have imposed.

I thought back to the iron hand my father had once wielded. The lads had jumped to what he said, the apprentices had scurried, and indeed I had wasted no time, but I could not remember that anyone had held him in actual physical fear.

I looked at Barty and faintly shivered. I wouldn't have liked to work under him, any more than Arknold's lads did.

"This is Tables Turned," Arknold was saying, approaching the box door of a dark chestnut colt. "One of Mrs. Cavesey's. Running at Germiston on Saturday."

"I thought I might go to Germiston," I said.

"Great," Danilo said with enthusiasm.

Arknold nodded more moderately, and said he would arrange for me to pick up free entrance tickets at the gate

We went into the box and stood in the usual sort of appreciative pause, looking Tables Turned over from head to foot, while Arknold noted how he was looking compared with the day before and I thought of something not too uncomplimentary to say about him.

"Good neck," I said. "Good strong shoulders." And a bit ratlike about the head, I thought.

Arknold shrugged heavily. "I took him down to Natal for the winter season, along with all the others. Had nearly the whole string down there for getting on for three months, like we do every year. We keep them at Summerveld, do you see?"

"Where is Summerveld?" I asked.

"More like *what* is Summerveld," he said. "It's a large area with stabling for about eight hundred horses, at Shongweni, near Durban. We book a block of stables there for the season. They have everything in the area one could need—practice track, restaurants, hostels for the boys, everything. And the school for jockeys and apprentices is there, as well."

"But you didn't do much good this year?" I said sympathetically.

"We won a few races with the others, but Mrs. Cavesey's string . . . Well, to be frank, there are so many of hers that I can't afford to have them all go wrong. Does my reputation no good, do you see?"

I did see. I also thought he spoke with less passion than he might have done.

"This Tables Turned," he said, slapping the horse's rump, "on his breeding and his early form, he looked a pretty good prospect for the Hollis Memorial Plate in June—that's one of the top two-year-old races—and he ran just like you saw Chink do at Newmarket. Blew up five hundred meters from home and finished exhausted, though I'd have sworn he was as fit as any of them."

He nodded to the boy holding the horse's head, turned on his heel, and strode out of the box. Farther down the line, we reached another of Nerissa's, who evoked an even deeper display of disgust.

"Now this colt, Medic, he should have been a proper worldbeater. I thought once that he'd win the Natal Free Handicap in July, but in the end I never sent him to Clairwood at all. His four races before that were too shameful."

I had a strong feeling that his anger was half genuine. It puzzled me. He certainly did seem to care that the horses had all failed, yet I was still sure that he not only knew why they had but had engineered it himself.

With Barty in attendance, pointing out omissions with a stabbing black forefinger to every intimidated stableboy, we finished inspecting all of the string, and afterward went across to the house for a drink.

"All of Mrs. Cavesey's lot are now counted as three-year-olds, of course," Arknold said. "The date for the age change out here is August 1st, not January 1st as with you."

"Yes," I said.

"There isn't much good racing here on the Rand tracks during August. Nothing much to interest you, I daresay.'

"I find it all extremely interesting," I said truthfully. "Will you go on running Mrs. Cavesey's string as three-year-olds?"

"As long as she cares to go on paying their training fees," he said gloomily.

"And if she decides to sell?"

"She'd get very little for them now."

"If she sold them, would you buy any of them?" I asked.

He didn't answer immediately, as he was showing us the way into his office, a square room full of papers, form books, filing cabinets, and hard upright chairs. Arknold's guests were not, it seemed, to be made so comfortable that they outstayed their limited welcome.

I repeated my question unwisely, and received the full glare of the Arknold displeasure.

"Look, Mister," he said fiercely, "I don't like what you're suggesting. You are saying that maybe I lose races so I can buy the horses cheap, then win races when I have them myself, and then sell them well for stud. That's what you're saying, Mister."

"I didn't say anything of the sort," I protested mildly.

"It's what you were thinking."

"Well," I said, "it was a possibility. Looking at it from outside, objectively, wouldn't that have occurred to you, too?"

He still glowered, but the antagonism slowly subsided. I wished I could decide whether he had been angry because I had insulted him, or because I had come too near the truth.

Danilo, who had been tagging along all the way making sunny comments to no one in particular, tried to smooth his ruffled friend.

"Aw, c'mon, Greville, he meant no harm."

Arknold gave me a sour look.

"Hey, c'mon. Aunt Nerissa probably told him to poke around for reasons, if he got the chance. You can't blame her when she's pouring all that good money into bad horses, now, can you, Greville?"

Arknold made a fair pretense at being pacified and offered us a drink. Danilo smiled hugely in relief and said it wouldn't do, it wouldn't do at all, for us to quarrel.

I sipped my drink and looked at the two of them.

Glossy young golden boy. Square surly middle-aged man. They both drank, and watched me over the rims of the glasses.

I couldn't see an inch into either of their souls.

Back at the Iguana Rock, there was a hand-delivered letter waiting for me. I read it upstairs in my room, standing by the window which looked out over the gardens, the tennis courts, and the great African outdoors. The light had begun fading and would soon go quickly, but the positive handwriting was still easy to see.

> Dear Mr. Lincoln,
>
> I have received a cable from Nerissa Cavesey asking me to invite you to dinner. My wife and I would be pleased to entertain you during your visit, if you would care to accept.
>
> Nerissa is the sister of my late brother's wife, Portia, and has become close to us through her visits to our country. I explain this, as Mr. Clifford Wenkins of Worldic Cinemas, who very reluctantly informed me of your whereabouts, was most insistent that you would not welcome any private invitations.
>
> Yours sincerely,
> Quentin van Huren

Behind the stiffly polite sentences, one could feel the irritation with which he had written that note. It was not only I, it seemed, who would do things slightly against his will for Nerissa's sake; and Clifford Wenkins, with his fussing misjudgment of his responsibilities, had clearly not improved the situation.

I went over to the telephone beside the bed and put a call through to the number printed alongside the address on the writing paper.

The call was answered by a black voice—a woman, who said she would see if Mr. van Huren was home.

Mr. van Huren decided he was.

"I called to thank you for your letter," I said. "And to

say that I would very much like to accept your invitation to dine with you during my stay." Two, I reckoned, could be ultra-polite.

His voice was as firm as his handwriting, and equally reserved.

"Good." He didn't sound overjoyed, however. "It is always a pleasure to please Nerissa."

"Yes," I said.

There was a pause. The conversation could hardly be said to be rocketing along at a scintillating rate.

I said helpfully, "I shall be here until a week next Wednesday."

"I see. Yes. However, I shall be away from home all next week, and we are already engaged this Saturday and Sunday."

"Then please don't worry," I said.

He cleared his throat. "I suppose," he suggested doubtfully, "that you would not be free tomorrow? Or, indeed, this evening? My house is not far from the Iguana Rock . . . but of course I expect you are fully engaged."

Tomorrow morning, I thought, all the newspapers would be flourishing a paragraph or two about Roderick Hodge's girl friend. By tomorrow night, Mrs. van Huren, if she felt like it, could fill her house with the sort of party I didn't like to go to. And tomorrow night I had agreed to have dinner with Conrad, though I could change that if I had to.

I said, "If it is not too short notice, tonight would be fine."

"Very well, then. Shall we say eight o'clock? I'll send my car to fetch you."

I put down the receiver half regretting that I had said I would go, as his pleasure in my acceptance was about as intense as a rice pudding. However, the alternatives seemed to be the same as the night before: either dine in the Iguana Rock restaurant, with the sidewise glances reaching me from the other tables, or upstairs alone in my room, wishing I was home with Charlie.

The house to which the van Hurens' car took me was

big, old, and spelled money from the marble doorstep onward. The hall was large, with the ceiling soaring away
into invisibility, and round all four sides there was a
graceful colonnade of pillars and arches: it looked like a
small, splendid Italian piazza, with a roof somewhere over
the top.

Into the hall, from a door under the colonnade on the
far side, came a man and a woman.

"I am Quentin van Huren," he said. "And this is my
wife, Vivi."

"How do you do?" I said politely, and shook their
hands.

There was a small hiatus.

"Yes . . . well," he said, making a gesture which was
very nearly a shrug. "Come along in."

I followed them into the room they had come from. In
the clearer light there, Quentin van Huren was instantly
identifiable as a serious man of substance, since about him
clung that unmistakable aura of know-how, experience,
and ability that constitutes true authority. As solidity and
professionalism were qualities I felt at home with, I was
immediately prepared to like him more than it seemed
probable he would like me.

His wife, Vivi, was not the same: elegant-looking, but
not in the same league intellectually.

She said, "Do sit down, Mr. Lincoln. We are so pleased
you could come. Nerissa is such a very dear friend. . . ."

She had cool eyes and a highly practiced social manner.
There was less warmth in her voice than in her words.
"Whiskey?" van Huren asked, and I said "Thank you,"
and got the tumblerful of water with the tablespoon of
Scotch.

"I'm afraid I haven't seen any of your films," van
Huren said, without sounding in the least sorry about it,
and his wife added, "We seldom go to the cinema."

"Very wise," I said without inflection, and neither of
them knew quite how to take it.

I found it easier on the whole to deal with people intent

on taking me down a peg rather than with sycophantic types. Toward the snubbers I felt no obligation.

I sat down on the gold-brocaded sofa which she had indicated, and sipped my enervated drink.

"Has Nerissa told you she is . . . ill?" I asked.

They both sat without haste. Van Huren shifted a small cushion out of his way, twisting in his armchair to see what he was doing, and answered over his shoulder.

"She wrote a little while ago. She said she had something wrong with her glands."

"She's dying," I said flatly, and got from them their first genuine response. They stopped thinking about me. Thought about Nerissa. About themselves. The shock and regret in their faces was real.

Van Huren still held the cushion in his hand.

"Are you sure?" he said.

I nodded. "She told me herself. A month or two, she says, is all she has."

"Oh, no," Vivi said, her grief showing through the social gloss like a thistle among orchids.

"I can't believe it," van Huren exclaimed. "She is always so full of life. So gay. So vital."

I thought of Nerissa as I had left her: vitality gone and life itself draining away.

"She is worried about her race horses," I said. "The ones Portia left her."

Neither of them was ready to think about race horses. Van Huren shook his head, finished putting the cushion comfortably in his chair, and stared into space. He was a well-built man, at a guess in his fifties, with hair going neatly gray in distinguished wings above his ears. Seen in profile, his nose was strongly rounded outward from the bridge, but stopped straight and short with no impression of a hook. He had a firm, full-lipped, well-defined mouth, hands with square well-manicured nails, and a dark gray suit over which someone had taken a lot of trouble.

The door from the hall opened suddenly and a boy and a girl, quite remarkably alike, came in. He, about twenty, had the slightly sullen air of one whose feelings of rebellion had not carried him as far as actually leaving his palatial home. She, about fifteen, had the uncomplicated directness of one to whom the idea of rebellion had not yet occurred.

"Oh, sorry," she said. "Didn't know we had anyone for dinner." She came across the room in her jeans and a pale yellow T-shirt, with her brother behind her dressed very much the same.

Van Huren said, "This is my son, Jonathan, and my daughter, Sally."

I stood up to shake hands with the girl, which seemed to amuse her.

"I say," she said. "Did anyone ever tell you you look like Edward Lincoln?"

"Yes," I said. "I am."

"You are what?"

"Edward Lincoln."

"Oh, yeah." She took a closer look. "Oh, golly. Good heavens. So you are." Then doubtfully, afraid I was making a fool of her, "Are you really?"

Her father said, "Mr. Lincoln is a friend of Mrs. Cavesey."

"Aunt Nerissa! Oh, yes. She told us once that she knew you well. She's such a darling, isn't she?"

"She is," I agreed, sitting down again.

Jonathan looked at me steadily with a cold and unimpressed eye.

"I never go to see your sort of film," he stated.

I smiled mildly and made no answer; it was typical of the putting-down brand of remark made to me with varying degrees of aggression almost every week of my life. Experience had long ago shown that the only unprovocative reply was silence.

"Well, I do," Sally said. "I've seen quite a few of them. Was it really you riding that horse in *Spy Across Country*, like the posters said?"

I nodded. "Mm."

She looked at me consideringly. "Wouldn't you have found it easier in a hackamore?"

I laughed involuntarily. "Well, no. I know the script said the horse had a very light mouth, but the one they actually gave me to ride had a hard one."

"Sally is a great little horsewoman," her mother said unnecessarily. "She won the big-pony class at the Rand Easter Show."

"On Rojedda Reef," Sally added.

The name meant nothing to me. But the others clearly thought it would. They looked at me expectantly, and in the end it was Jonathan who said with superiority, "It's the name of our gold mine."

"Really? I didn't know you had a gold mine." I half deliberately said it with the same inflection that father and son had said they didn't see my films, and Quentin van Huren heard it. He turned his head quite sharply toward me, and I could feel the internal smile coming out of my eyes.

"Yes," he said thoughtfully, holding my gaze. "I see." His lips twitched. "Would you care to go down one? To see what goes on?"

From the surprised expressions on the rest of his family, I gathered that what he had offered was more or less the equivalent of my suggesting a press conference.

"I'd like it enormously," I assured him. "I really would."

"I'm flying down to Welkom on Monday morning," he said. "That's the town where Rojedda is. I'll be there the whole week, but if you care to come down with me Monday, you can fly back again the same evening."

I said that that would be great.

By the end of dinner, the van Huren-Lincoln entente had progressed to the point where three of the family decided to go to Germiston that Saturday to watch Nerissa's horses run. Jonathan said he had more important things to do.

"Like what?" Sally demanded.

Jonathan didn't really know.

7

Friday turned out to be a meager day for world news, which left a lot too much space for the perils of Katya. Seldom had the press been invited in advance to such a spectacle, and in most papers it seemed to have made the front page.

One of them first unkindly suggested that it had all been a publicity stunt which had gone wrong, and then denied it most unconvincingly in the following paragraph.

I wondered, reading it, how many people would believe just that. I wondered, remembering that mischievous smile, whether Katya could possibly even have set it up herself. She and Roderick, between them.

But she wouldn't have risked her life. Not unless she hadn't realized she was risking it.

I picked up the Rand *Daily Star* to see what they had made of Roderick's information, and found that he had written the piece himself. "By our own Rand *Daily Star* eyewitness, Roderick Hodge," it announced at the top. Considering his emotional involvement, it was not too highly colored, but it was he, more than any of the others, who stressed, as Conrad had done, that if Katya had not taken the microphone away from me, it would have been I who got the shock.

I wondered how much Roderick wished I had. For one thing, it would have made a better story.

With a twisting smile, I read on to the end. Katya, he reported finally, was being detained in hospital overnight, her condition described as "comfortable."

I shoved the papers aside, and while I showered and shaved came to two conclusions. One was that what I had done was not particularly remarkable and certainly not worth the coverage, and the other was that after this I was going to have even more trouble explaining to Nerissa why all I could bring her were guesses, not proof.

Down at the reception desk, I asked if they could get me a packed lunch and hire me a horse for the day out in some decent riding country. Certainly, they said, and waved a few magic wands; by midmorning I was twenty-five miles north of Johannesburg setting out along a dirt road in brilliant sunshine on a pensioned-off race horse who had seen better days. I took a deep contented breath of the sweet smell of Africa and padded along with a great feeling of freedom. The people who owned the horse had gently insisted on sending their head boy along with me so that I shouldn't get lost, but as he spoke little English and I no Bantu, I found him a most peaceful companion. George was small, rode well, and had a great line in banana-shaped smiles.

We passed a crossroads where there was stall, all by itself, loaded with bright orange fruit and festooned with pineapples, with one man beaming beside them.

"Naartjies," George said, pointing.

I made signs that I didn't understand. One thing about being an actor, it occasionally came in useful.

"Naartjies," George repeated, dismounting from his horse and leading it toward the stall. I grasped the fact that George wanted to buy, so I called to him and fished out a five-rand note. George smiled, negotiated rapidly, and returned with a huge string bag of naartjies, two ripe pineapples, and most of the money.

In easy undemanding companionship, we rode farther, dismounted in some shade, ate a pineapple each, and cold chicken from the Iguana Rock, and drank some refreshing unsweet apple juice from tins George had been given to bring along. The naartjies turned out to be like large lumpy tangerines with green patches on the skin; they also tasted like tangerines, but better.

George ate his lunch thirty feet away from me. I beckoned to him to come closer, but he wouldn't.

In the afternoon, we trotted and cantered a long way over tough scrubby brown dried grass, and finally, walking to cool the horses, found ourselves approaching the home stables from the opposite direction to the way we set out.

They asked ten rand for the hire of the horse, though the day I had had was worth a thousand, and I gave George five rand for himself, which his employer whispered was too much. George, with a last dazzling smile, handed me the bag of naartjies and they all gave me friendly waves when I left. If only life were all so natural, so undemanding, so unfettered.

Five miles down the road, I reflected that if it were I would be bored to death.

Conrad was before me at the Iguana.

He met me as I came into the hall, and surveyed me from head to foot—dust, sweat, naartjies, and all.

"What on earth have you been doing, dear boy?"

"Riding."

"What a pity I haven't an Arriflex with me," he exclaimed. "What a shot—you standing there looking like a gypsy with your back to the light, and those oranges—have to work it into our next film together. Can't waste a shot like that."

"You're early," I remarked.

"Might as well wait here as anywhere else."

"Come upstairs, then, while I change."

He came up to my room and with unfailing instinct chose the most comfortable chair.

"Have a naartjie," I said.

"I'd rather have a Martini, dear boy."

"Order one, then."

He rang for his drink and it came while I was in the shower. I toweled dry and went back into the bedroom in underpants to find him equipped also with a Churchill-sized cigar, wreathed in smoke and smelling of London clubs and plutocracy. He was looking through the pile of newspapers which still lay tidily on the table, but in the end he left them undisturbed.

"I've seen all those," he said. "How do you like being a real hero, for a change?"

"Don't be nutty. What's so heroic about first aid?"

He grinned. Changed the subject.

"What in hell's name made you come out here for a première after all those years of refusing to show your face off the screen?"

"I came to see some horses," I said, and explained about Nerissa.

"Oh, well, then, dear boy, that does make more sense, I agree. And have you found out what's wrong?"

I shrugged. "Not really. Don't see how I can." I fished out a clean shirt and buttoned it on. "I'm going to Germiston races tomorrow, and I'll keep my eyes open again, but I doubt if anyone could ever prove anything against Greville Arnold." I put on some socks and dark blue trousers, and some slip-on shoes. "What are you and Evan doing here, anyway?"

"Film-making. What else?"

"What film?"

"Some Goddam awful story about elephants that Evan took it into his head to do. It was all set up before he got roped in to finish *Man in a Car*, and since he chose to ponce around in Spain for all that time, we were late getting out here. Should be down in the Kruger Game Park by now."

I brushed my hair.

"Who's playing the lead?"

"Drix Goddart."

I glanced at Conrad over my shoulder. He smiled sardonically. "Wax in Evan's hands, dear boy. Laps up direction like a well-patted puppy."

"Nice for you all."

"He's so neurotic that if someone doesn't tell him every five minutes he's brilliant, he thinks everyone hates him."

"Is he here with you?"

"No, thank God. He was supposed to be, but now he comes out with all the rest of the team after Evan and I have sorted out which locations we want to use."

I put down the brushes and fastened my watch round my wrist. Keys, change, handkerchief into trouser pockets.

"Did you see the rushes of the desert scenes while you were in England?" Conrad asked.

"No," I said. "Evan didn't invite me."

"Just like him." He took a long swallow and rolled the Martini round his teeth. He squinted at the long ash on the end of his mini-torpedo. He said, "They were good."

"So they damn well ought to be. We did them enough times."

He smiled without looking at me. "You won't like the finished film."

After a pause, as he didn't explain, I said, "Why not?"

"There's something in it besides and beyond acting." He paused again, considering his words. "Even to a jaundiced eye like mine, dear boy, the quality of suffering is shattering."

I didn't say anything. He swiveled his eyes in my direction.

"Usually you do not reveal much of yourself, do you? Well, this time, dear boy, this time . . ."

I compressed my lips. I knew what I'd done. I'd known while I did it. I had just hoped that no one would be perceptive enough to notice.

"Will the critics see what you saw?" I asked.

He smiled lopsidedly. "Bound to, aren't they? The best ones, anyway."

I stared despondently at the carpet. The trouble with interpreting scenes too well, with taking an emotion and making the audience feel it sharply, was that it meant stripping oneself naked in public. Nothing as simple as naked skin, but letting the whole world peer into one's mind, one's beliefs, one's experience.

To be able to reproduce a feeling so that others could recognize it, and perhaps understand it for the first time, one had to have some idea of what it felt like in reality. To show that one knew meant revealing what one had felt. Revealing oneself too nakedly did not come easily to a private man, and if one did not reveal oneself, one never became a great actor.

I was not a great actor. I was competent and popular, but unless I wholeheartedly took the step into frightening personal exposure, I would never do anything great. There was always for me, in acting beyond a certain limit, an element of mental distress. But I had thought, when I risked doing it in the car, that my own self would be merged indiscernibly with the trials the fictional character was enduring.

I had done it because of Evan: to spite him, more than to please him. There was a point beyond which no director could claim credit for an actor's performance, and I had gone a long way beyond that point.

"What are you thinking?" Conrad demanded.

"I was deciding to stick exclusively in future to unreal entertaining escapades, as in the past."

"You're a coward, dear boy."

"Yes."

He tapped the ash off his cigar.

"No one is going to be satisfied if you do."

"Of course they are."

"Uh-uh." He shook his head. "No one will settle for paste after they see they could have the real thing."

"Stop drinking Martinis," I said. "They give you rotten ideas."

I walked across the room, picked up my jacket, put it on, and stowed my wallet and diary inside it.

"Let's go down to the bar," I said.

He levered himself obediently out of the chair.

"You can't run away from yourself forever, dear boy."

"I'm not the man you think I am."

"Oh, yes," Conrad said. "Dear boy, you are."

At Germiston races the next day, I found waiting for me at the gate not only the free entrance tickets promised by Greville Arknold, but also a racecourse official with a duplicate set and instructions to take me up to lunch with the Chairman of the Race Club.

I meekly followed where he led, and was presently shown into a large dining room where about a hundred people were already eating at long tables. The whole van Huren family, including a sulky Jonathan, occupied chairs near the end of the table closest to the door, and when he saw me come in, van Huren himself rose to his feet.

"Mr. Klugvoigt, this is Edward Lincoln," he said to the man sitting at the end of the table, and to me added, "Mr. Klugvoigt is the Chairman."

Klugvoigt stood up, shook hands, indicated the empty chair on his left, and we all sat down.

Vivi van Huren in a sweeping green hat sat opposite me, on the Chairman's right, with her husband beside her. Sally van Huren was on my left, with her brother beyond. They all seemed to know Klugvoigt well, and as a personality he had much in common with van Huren: same air of wealth and substance, same self-confidence, same bulk of body and acuity of mind.

Once past the preliminaries and the politenesses (How did I like South Africa? Nowhere so comfortable as the Iguana Rock. How long was I staying?), the conversation veered naturally back to the chief matter in hand.

Horses.

The van Hurens owned a four-year-old which had finished third in the Dunlop Gold Cup a month earlier, but they were giving it a breather during these less important months. Klugvoigt owned two three-year-olds running that afternoon, with nothing much expected.

I steered the conversation round to Nerissa's horses without much difficulty, and from there to Greville

Arknold, asking, but not pointedly, how he was in general regarded, both as man and trainer.

Neither van Huren nor Klugvoigt was of the kind to come straight out with what he thought. It was Jonathan who leaned forward and let out the jet of truth.

"He's a rude bloody bastard, with hands as heavy as a gold brick."

"I have to advise Nerissa when I get home," I commented.

"Aunt Portia always said he had a way with horses," Sally objected, in defense.

"Yeah. Backwards," said Jonathan.

Van Huren gave him a flickering glance in which humor was by no means lacking, but he changed the subject immediately with the expertise of one thoroughly awake to the risk of slander.

"Your Clifford Wenkins, Link, telephoned to me yesterday afternoon to offer us all some tickets to your première." He looked amused. I gratefully accepted that he had loosened with me to the point of dropping the meticulous "Mr." and thought that in an hour or two I might get around to "Quentin."

"Apparently he had had second thoughts about his abruptness to me when I asked for your address."

"Probably been doing some belated homework," agreed Klugvoigt, who seemed to know all about it.

"It's only a—an adventure film," I said. "You might not enjoy it."

He gave me a dry sardonic smile. "You won't accuse me again of condemning what I haven't seen."

I smiled back. I considerably liked Nerissa's sister's husband's brother.

We finished an excellent lunch and wandered out for the first race. Horses were already being mounted, and Vivi and Sally hurried off to upset the odds with a couple of rand.

"Your friend Wenkins said he would be here today," van Huren remarked.

"Oh, dear."

He chuckled.

Arknold, in the parade ring, was throwing his magenta-shirted jockey up into the saddle.

"How heavy is a gold brick?" I asked.

Van Huren followed my gaze. "Seventy-two pounds, usually. You can't lift them as easily, though, as seventy-two pounds of jockey."

Danilo was standing by the rails, watching. He turned as the mounted horses walked away, caught sight of us, and came straight across.

"Hi, Link. I've been looking out for you. How's about a beer?"

I said, "Quentin" (not two hours: ten minutes), "this is Danilo Cavesey, Nerissa's nephew. And, Danilo, this is Quentin van Huren, whose sister-in-law Portia van Huren was Nerissa's sister."

"Gee," Danilo said. His eyes widened and stayed wide, without blinking. He was more than ordinarily surprised.

"Good heavens," van Huren exclaimed. "I didn't even know she had a nephew."

"I kinda dropped out of her life when I was about six, I guess," Danilo said. "I only saw her again this summer, when I was over in England from the States."

Van Huren said he had only twice met Nerissa's husband, and never his brother, Danilo's father. Danilo said he had never met Portia. The two of them sorted out the family ramifications to their own content and seemed to meet in understanding in a very short time.

"Well, what do you know?" Danilo said, evidently pleased to the roots. "Say, isn't that just too much?"

When Vivi and Sally and Jonathan rejoined us after the race, they chattered about it like birds, waving their arms about and lifting their voices in little whoops.

"He's a sort of cousin," said Sally positively. "Isn't it the greatest fun?"

Even Jonathan seemed to brighten up at the idea of receiving the sunshine kid into the family, and the two of them presently bore him away on their own. I saw him looking back over his shoulder with a glance for me that was a lot older than anything Jonathan or Sally could produce.

"What a nice boy," Vivi said.

"Nerissa is very fond of him," I agreed.

"We must ask him over while he is here, don't you think, Quentin? Oh, look, do you see who's down there—Janet Frankenloots—haven't seen her for ages. Oh, do excuse me, Link. . . ." The great hat swooped off to meet the long-lost friend.

Van Huren was too depressingly right about Clifford Wenkins being at the races. To say that the Distribution Manager approached as directly as Danilo had done would be inaccurate: he made a crabwise deprecating semicircle, tripping over his feet, and ended damply by my side.

"Er—Link, good to see you. . . . Er, would you be Mr. van Huren? Pleased—er—to meet you, sir."

He shook hands with van Huren, who from long social practice managed not to wipe his palm on his trousers afterward.

"Now. Er—Link. I've tried to reach you a couple of times, but you never seem er—I mean—I haven't called you when you are—er—in. So I thought—well, I mean, er—I would be certain to see you here."

I waited without much patience. He pulled a batch of paper hastily out of an inside pocket.

"Now, we want—that is to say, Worldic have arranged—er, since you did the press interviews, I mean—they want you to go to—let's see. . . . There's a beauty competition to judge next Wednesday for Miss Jo'burg—and, er, guest of honor at the ladies' Kinema Luncheon Club on Thursday—and on Friday a fund-raising charity reception given by—er, our sponsors for the première—er, that is, Bow-Miouw Pet Food, of course, and, er—well, Saturday's the official opening of, er—the Modern Homes Exhibition. All good publicity—er—"

"No," I said. And for hell's sake don't lose your temper here, I told myself severely.

"Er," Wenkins said, seeing no danger signals. "We—er,

that is, Worldic, do think—I mean—that you really ought to cooperate."

"Oh, they do." I slowed my breathing deliberately. "Why do you think I won't let Worldic pay my expenses? Why do you think I pay for everything myself?"

He was extremely unhappy. Worldic must have been putting on the pressure from one side, and now I was resisting him from the other. The beads sprang out on his forehead.

"Yes, but—" He swallowed. "Well—I expect—I mean—the various organizatons might be prepared to offer—er, I mean—well, *fees*."

I counted five. Squeezed my eyes shut and opened them. Said, when I was sure it would come out moderately, "Mr. Wenkins, you can tell Worldic that I do not wish to accept any of those invitations. In fact, I will go only to the première itself and a simple reception before or after, as I said."

"But . . . we have told everybody that you will."

"You know that my agent particularly asked you, right at the beginning, not to fix anything at all."

"Yes, but Worldic say—I mean—"

Stuff Worldic, I thought violently. I said, "I'm not going to do those things."

"But—you can't—I mean—*disappoint* them all—not now. They will not go to your films if you don't turn up when—er, we've—er, well—promised you will."

"You will have to tell them that you committed me without asking me first."

"Worldic won't like it."

"They won't like it because it will hurt their own takings, if it hurts anything at all. But it's their own fault. If they thought they could make me go to those functions by a species of blackmail, they were wrong."

Clifford Wenkins was looking at me anxiously and van Huren with some curiosity, and I knew that despite my best intentions the anger was showing through.

I took pity on Clifford Wenkins and a grip on myself. "Tell Worldic I will not be in Johannesburg at all next week. Tell them that if they had had the common sense to check with me first, I could have told them I am committed elsewhere, until the première."

He swallowed again and looked even unhappier.

"They said I must persuade you."

"I'm sorry."

"They might even fire me."

"Even for you, Mr. Wenkins, I can't do it. I won't be here."

He gave me a spanked-spaniel look which I didn't find endearing, and when I said no more he turned disgustedly away and walked off, stuffing the papers roughly into the side pocket of his jacket.

Van Huren turned his handsome head and gave me an assessing look.

"Why did you refuse him?" he asked. No blame in his voice; simply interest.

I took a deep breath, got the rueful smile out, and stifled the irritation which Clifford Wenkins had raised like an allergic rash.

"I never do those things—beauty contests and lunches and opening things."

"Yes. But why not?"

"I haven't the stamina."

"You're big enough," he said.

I smiled and shook my head. It would have sounded pretentious to tell him that so-called "personal appearances" left me feeling invaded, battered, and devoured, and that complimentary introductory speeches gave me nothing in return. The only compliment I truly appreciated was the money plonked down at the box office.

"Where are you off to next week, then?" he asked.

"Africa is huge," I said, and he laughed.

We wandered back to look at the next batch of hopefuls in the parade ring, and identified number eight as Nerissa's filly Lebona.

"She looks perfectly all right," van Huren commented.

"She will start all right," I agreed. "And run well for three-quarters of the way. Then she'll tire suddenly within a few strides and drop right out, and when she comes back her sides will be heaving and she'll look exhausted."

He was startled. "You sound as if you know all about it."

"Only guessing. I saw Chink run like that at Newmarket on Wednesday."

"But you think they are all running to the same pattern?"

"The form book confirms it."

"What will you tell Nerissa, then?"

I shrugged. "I don't know. . . . Probably to change her trainer."

In due course, we returned to the stands and watched Lebona run as expected. Van Huren seeming in no haste to jettison me for more stimulating company, and I well content to have him as a buffer state, the two of us, passing the cluster of tables and chairs under sun umbrellas, decided to sit down there and order refreshers.

For the first day since I had arrived, the sunshine had grown hot. No breeze stirred the fringes round the flowered umbrellas, and ladies in all directions were shedding their coats.

Van Huren, however, sighed when I commented on the good weather.

"I like winter best," he said. "When it's cold, dry, and sunny. The summers are wet, and far too hot, even up here on the highveld."

"One thinks of South Africa as always being hot."

"It is, of course. Once you get down near to sea level, it can be scorching even as early as this."

The shadows of two men fell across the table, and we both looked up.

Two men I knew. Conrad; and Evan Pentelow.

I made introductions, and they pulled up chairs and joined us: Conrad his usual flamboyant self, scattering "dear boy"s with abandon; and Evan, hair as unruly as ever, and eyes as hot.

Evan weighed straight in. "You won't now refuse to turn up at the première of my *Man in a Car,* I hope."

"You sound very proprietary," I said mildly. "It isn't altogether yours."

"My name will come first in the credits," he asserted aggressively.

"Before mine?"

Posters of Evan's films were apt to have "EVAN PENTELOW" in large letters at the top, followed by the name of the film, followed, in the last third of the space, by the actors' names all squashed closely together. Piracy, it was, or little short.

Evan glared, and I guessed he had checked my contract for the film, and found, as I had done, that in the matter of billing my agent had made no mistakes.

"Before the other director," he said grudgingly.

I supposed that was fair. Although he had directed less than a quarter, the shape of the finished film would be his idea.

Van Huren followed the sparring with amusement and attention.

"So billing does matter as much as they say."

"It depends"—I smiled—"on who is sticking knives into whose back."

Evan had no sense of humor and was not amused. He began instead to talk about the film he was going to make next.

"It's an allegory. . . . Every human scene is balanced by a similar one involving elephants. They were supposed to be the good guys of the action, originally, but I've been learning a thing or two about elephants. Did you know they are more dangerous to man than any other animal in Africa? Did you know that nothing preys on them except ivory hunters, and as ivory hunting is banned in the Kruger Park, the elephants are in the middle of a population explosion? They are increasing by a thousand a year, which means that in ten years there will be no room for any other animals, and probably no trees in the park, as the elephants uproot them by the hundred."

Evan, as usual on any subject which took his attention, was dogmatic and intense.

"And do you know," he went on, "that elephants don't like Volkswagens? Those small ones, I mean. Elephants seldom attack cars ordinarily, but they seem to make a beeline for Volkswagens."

Van Huren gave a disbelieving smile, which naturally stirred Evan to further passion.

"It's true! I might even incorporate it in the film."

"Should be interesting," Conrad said with more than a touch of dryness. "Leaving a car around as bait at least makes a change from goats and tigers."

Evan glanced at him sharply, but nodded. "We go down to the park on Wednesday."

Van Huren turned to me with a look of regret.

"What a pity you can't go down there, too, Link, next week. You want somewhere to go, and you'd have liked it there. The game reserves are about all that's left of the old natural Africa, and the Kruger is big and open and still pretty wild. But I know the accommodation there is always booked up months ahead."

I didn't think Evan would have wanted me in the least, but to my surprise he said slowly, "Well, as it happens, we made reservations for Drix Goddart to be down there with us, but now he's not coming for a week or two. We haven't cancelled. . . . There will be an empty bed, if you want to come."

I looked at Conrad in amazement but found no clue in his raised eyebrows and sardonic mouth.

If it hadn't been for Evan himself, I would have leaped at it; but I supposed that even he was a great deal preferable to Clifford Wenkins's program. And if I didn't go to the Kruger, which very much appealed to me, where else?

"I'd like to," I said. "And thanks."

8

Danilo fetched up at the sunshade flanked by his two van Huren satellites.

Sally waited for no introductions to Conrad and Evan. She looked to see that she was not actually interrupting anyone in midsentence, and then spoke directly to her father.

"We told Danilo you were taking Link down the gold mine on Monday, and he wants to know if he could go, too."

Danilo looked slightly embarrassed to have his request put so baldly, but after only a fraction's hesitation van Huren said, "Why, of course, Danilo, if you would like to."

"I sure would," he said earnestly.

"Gold mine?" said Evan intently, pouncing on the words.

"The family business," explained van Huren, and scattered introductions all round.

"There could be great background material. . . . A gold mine . . . something I could use one day." He looked expectantly at van Huren, who was thus landed unfairly with the choice of being coerced or ungracious. He took it in his stride.

"By all means, join us on Monday if you would care to."

Evan gave him no chance to retract, and included Conrad in the deal.

When they and the three young ones had all gone off to place their bets, I apologized to van Huren that his generosity should have been stretched.

He shook his head. "It will be all right. We seldom take large parties of visitors down the mine, as it slows or stops production too much, but we can manage four of you without a break in work, if you are all sensible, as I am sure you will be."

By the end of the afternoon, the number had grown to five; Roderick Hodge also turned up at Germiston and, having learned of the expedition, begged van Huren privately to be allowed to tag along, with a view to a feature article in the Rand *Daily Star*.

I would have thought that gold mines were a stale topic in Johannesburg, but Roderick had his way.

I found him unexpectedly at my elbow while I was watching Tables Turned amble round the parade ring looking the prize colt he was not. Danilo and all the van Hurens had gone to take tea with the Chairman, a meal I preferred to do without, and Conrad and Evan were away in the distance being accosted by the ever-perspiring Clifford.

Roderick touched me on the arm, and said tentatively, "Link?"

I turned. His fortyish face had grown new lines in the last few days and looked much too old for the length of his trendy hair and the boyish cut of his clothes.

"How is Katya?" I asked.

"She's fine. Remarkable, really."

I said I was glad, and then asked if he often went to the races.

"No. . . . Actually, I came to see you. I tried to get you at the Iguana Rock, but they said you were at the races."

"Did they indeed," I murmured.

"I have what you might call a *source* there," he explained. "Keeps me informed, you see."

I saw. All over the world, there was a gray little army which tipped off the press and got tipped in return: hotel porters, railway porters, hospital porters, and anyone within earshot of V.I.P. lounges at airports.

"I live this side of the city, so I thought I might just as well drift along."

"A nice day," I said.

He looked up at the sky as if it would have been all one to him if it had been snowing.

"I suppose so. . . . Look, I got a call this morning from Joe—that's the chap who was setting up the radio equipment at Randfontein House."

"I remember," I said.

"He said he had taken that microphone to pieces, and there was nothing wrong with it. The outer wire of the coaxial cable was of course connected to the metal casing, though—"

"Ah," I interrupted. "And what exactly is a coaxial cable?"

"Don't you know? It's an electric cable made of two wires, but one wire goes up the center like a core, and the other wire is circular, outside it. Television aerial cables are coaxial. You can see that by the ends, where you plug them into the sets."

"Oh, yes," I said. "I see."

"Joe says he found the earth wire and the live wire had been fastened to the wrong terminals in the power plug of the recorder he was using for Katya. He says people are warned over and over again about the dangers of doing that, but they still do it. The current would go straight through the mike's casing, and earth itself through whoever was holding it."

I thought. "Wouldn't the whole recorder have been live, too?"

He blinked. "Yes. Joe says that inside it must have been. But no one would have got a shock from it. The casing of the recorder was plastic, the knobs were plastic, and Joe himself was wearing rubber-soled shoes, which he says he always does anyway, as a precaution."

"But he must have used that recorder before," I protested.

"He says not. He says he plugged it in because it was just standing there when something went wrong with his own. He didn't know whose it was, and no one seems to have claimed it since."

Arknold gave his jockey a leg up onto Tables Turned, and the horses began to move out for the race.

I said, "It was all very bad luck."

"Joe thinks so," he said. There was, however, a shade of doubt in his voice and I looked at him inquiringly. "Well . . . it's an appalling thing to say, but Joe wondered whether it could possibly have been a publicity stunt that went too far. He says that Clifford Wenkins was fussing round the electronic equipment after your first broadcast, and that you yourself set up the conference, and you did get the most fantastic press coverage for saving Katya."

"I agree it's an appalling thing to say," I said cheerfully. "Consider me appalled. Consider also that I have already wondered whether it was a publicity stunt set up by you and Katya . . . which went too far."

He stared. Then relaxed. Then ruefully smiled.

"All right," he said. "Neither of us fixed it. How about our Clifford?"

"You know him better than I do," I said. "But although he seems to have sold his soul to Worldic Cinemas, he doesn't strike me as having the nerve or the ingenuity to fix it all up."

"You fluster him," Roderick observed. "He isn't always as futile-seeming as he's been since you arrived."

Farther along the rails from us stood Danilo, watching Nerissa's colt with a smile on his frank and bonny face. I thought that if he had known he was so soon to inherit them, he would have been anxious instead.

Arknold joined him, and together they walked onto the stands to watch. Roderick and I tailed along after. We all watched Tables Turned set off at a great rate, run out of puff two furlongs from home, and finish a spent force.

Arknold, muttering under his breath and looking like thunder, bumped into me as he made his way down the steps to hold a post-mortem with the jockey.

He focused on me and said abruptly, "It's too much, Mister. It's too much. That's a bloody good colt and he should have won by a mile in that company." He shut his mouth like a trap, brushed past me, and thrust his way down through the crowd.

"Whatever's all that about?" Roderick asked casually; so casually that I remembered the Rand *Daily Star,* and didn't tell him.

"No idea," I said, putting on a bit of puzzle, but Roderick's skeptical expression said that he similarly was remembering where I worked.

We walked down from the stands. I considered ways and means, and decided Klugvoigt was the best bet for what I wanted. So I drifted Roderick gently to where Conrad and Evan were discussing adjourning to the bar, inserted him into their notice, and left as he began telling Conrad the theories of Joe and the coaxial cable.

The Chairman was in his private box surrounded by ladies in decorative hats. He saw me hovering alone, beckoned to me to come up the adjacent stairs, and, when I reached his side, pressed into my hand some drowned whiskey in a warmish glass.

"How are you doing?" he asked. "Winning, I hope."

"Not losing, anyway." I smiled.

"What do you fancy in the next?"

"I'd have to see them in the parade ring first."

"Wise fellow," he agreed.

I admired the facilities. "The stands look new," I commented.

"Not long built," he said. "Very much needed, of course."

"And the weighing room—from the outside it looks so comfortable."

"Oh, it is, my dear chap." A thought struck him. "Would you care to see round inside it?"

"How very kind of you," I said warmly, and made ready-to-go-at-once movements so that he shouldn't forget. After a moment or two, we parked our unfinished drinks and strolled easily across to the large square administrative block which housed the weighing and changing rooms on the ground floor and the racecourse offices upstairs.

The whole thing was modern and comfortable, a long way from all too many English equivalents. There was a large room furnished with easy chairs where owners and trainers could sit in comfort to plan their coups and dissect their flops, but Klugvoigt whisked me past it into the inner recesses.

The jockeys themselves shared in the bonanza, being supplied with man-sized wire lockers for their clothes (instead of a peg), a sauna bath (as well as showers), and upholstered day beds to rest on (instead of a hard narrow wooden bench).

The man I had hoped to see was lying on one of the black leather-covered beds supporting himself on one elbow. He was known to me via the number boards as K. L. Fahrden. He was Greville Arknold's jockey.

I told Klugvoigt I would be interested to speak to him, and he said sure, go ahead, he would wait for me in the reception room by the door, as there was someone there he, too, wanted to speak with.

Fahrden had the usual sharp fine bones with the usual lack of fatty tissue between them and the skin. His wary, narrow-eyed manner changed a shade for the better when Klugvoigt told him my name, but underwent a relapse when I said I was a friend of Mrs. Cavesey.

"You can't blame me for her horses running so stinking," he said defensively.

"I don't," I said patiently. "I only wanted to ask you how they felt to you personally, so that I could tell Mrs. Cavesey what you said."

"Oh. Oh, well, then." He considered, and came across.

"They give you a good feel, see, at the start. Full of running, and reveling in it. Then you go to pick 'em up, see, and there's bloody nothing there. Put on the pressure, see, and they blow up instant like."

"You must have given them a lot of thought," I said. "What do you think is wrong with them?"

He gave me a sidelong look. "Search me," he said.

"You must have a theory," I urged.

"Only the same as anyone would," he said reluctantly. "And I'm not saying more than that."

"Mm. . . . Well, what do you think of Mr. Arknold's head lad?"

"Barty? That great brute. Can't say as I've even thought much about him. Wouldn't want to meet him alone on a dark night, if that's what you mean."

It wasn't entirely what I meant, but I let it go. I asked him instead how he got on with Danilo.

"A real nice guy, that," he said, with the first sign of friendliness. "Always takes a great interest in Arknold's horses, of course, seeing as how so many of them are his aunt's."

"Did you meet him when he was over here before?" I asked.

"Oh, sure. He stayed in the hotel down in Summerveld for a couple of weeks. A great guy. Always good for a laugh. He said he'd just been staying with his aunt, and she was a great girl. He was the only cheerful thing around when the horses started running badly."

"When was that?" I asked with sympathy in my voice.

"Oh, way back in June sometime. Since then, there's been every investigation you could think of into why they flop. Dope tests, vets, the lot."

"Is Arknold a good man to ride for?" I asked.

He closed up at once. "More than my job's worth to say different."

I fielded Klugvoigt from the reception room, thanked him, and walked back with him toward the parade ring. Someone buttonholed him on the way, so I wandered by myself right across the course to the simple stand of plain wooden steps on the far side. From there one had a comprehensive view of the whole layout: the long sweep of stands, the small patch of sun umbrellas, the block of private boxes. Behind them all, the parade ring and the weighing room.

And round and about, mingling, chatting, exchanging information, and sipping at cooling glasses, went Danilo and Arknold, Conrad and Evan, Roderick and Clifford Wenkins, and Quentin, Vivi, Jonathan, and Sally van Huren.

I booked a telephone call to Charlie when I got back to the Iguana Rock that evening, and it came through punctually the next morning, Sunday, at ten o'clock.

We could hear each other as if we had been six miles apart instead of six thousand. She said she was glad I had called and glad that I wasn't electrocuted: yes, she said, it had been in all the papers at home yesterday, and one or two disgustedly hinted that it had all been a put-up job.

"It wasn't," I said. "I'll tell you all about it when I get home. How are the kids?"

"Oh, fine. Chris says he's going to be an astronaut, and Libby has managed to say 'pool' when she wants to go in the water."

"That's great," I said, meaning Libby's advance, and Charlie said yes, it was great, it really was.

"I do miss you," I said lightly, and she answered with equal lack of intensity, "It seems a lot longer than five days since you went away."

"I'll be back straight after the première," I said. "Before that, I'm taking a look round a gold mine and then going to the Kruger National Park for a few days."

"Lucky sod."

"After the kids have gone back to school, we'll have a holiday somewhere, just by ourselves," I said.

"I'll hold you to it."

"You can choose, so start planning."

"O.K." She said it casually, but sounded pleased.

"Look . . . I really rang about Nerissa's horses."

"Have you found out what's wrong with them?"

"I don't know," I said. "But I have had a fairly cataclysmic idea. I can't be sure I'm right, though, until—or, in fact, unless—you can do something for me in England."

"Shoot," she said economically.

"I want you to take a look at Nerissa's will."

"Wow." She drew in a sharp breath. "How on earth do I do that?"

"Ask her. I don't know how you'll manage it, but if she's had fun drawing it up, she might not mind talking about it."

"Well, what exactly do you want me to look for if she lets me see it?"

"I want to know particularly if, besides the horses, she has left the residue of her estate to Danilo."

"All right," she said doubtfully. "Is it very important?"

"Yes and no." I half laughed. "Young Danilo is out here in South Africa at this moment."

"Is he?" she exclaimed. "Nerissa didn't tell us that."

"Nerissa doesn't know," I said. I described the golden Danilo to her, and also Arknold, and explained how the horses all lost to the same pattern.

"Sounds like the trainer nobbling them," she commented.

"Yes. I thought so, too, at first. But now—well, I think it's the California kid, our Danilo."

"But it can't be," she objected. "Whatever could he have to gain?"

"Death duties," I said. Emphatically.

After a pause, Charlie said doubtfully, "You can't mean it."

"I do mean it. It's a theory, anyway. But I can't begin to prove it."

"I don't really see . . ."

"Imagine," I said, "that when Danilo went to see Nerissa in the early summer, their first reunion after all those years, she told him she had Hodgkin's disease. He had only to look it up in a medical directory and he would find out it is always fatal."

"Oh, dear," she said, sighing. "Go on."

"Nerissa liked him very much," I said. "Well, he's an attractive boy in ways. Supposing that, after she'd decided to, she told Danilo she was leaving him her horses, and some money as well."

"It's an awful lot of supposing."

"Yes," I agreed. "Would you ask Nerissa? Ask her if she told Danilo what illness she had, and also if she told him what she was leaving him."

"Darling, she'd be terribly distressed, at this stage, to find she was wrong about him." Charlie herself sounded upset. "She is so very pleased to have him to leave things to."

"Just get her chatting on the subject, if you can, and ask her casually. I agree that it's important not to distress her. It might actually be better to let Danilo get away with it. In fact, I've been thinking about that for most of the night. He has been defrauding her of the prize money she might have won. How much would she mind?"

"She might even laugh. Like you did just now. She might even think it was a pretty bright idea."

"Yes. Of course he has also been defrauding the South African betting public, but I suppose it's up to the racing authorities here to deal with it, if they catch him."

"What makes you think it is Danilo?"

"It's so insubstantial," I said with frustration. "Mostly a matter of chance remarks and impressions, and terribly few facts. Well, for one thing, Danilo was around the horses when they started doing badly. Their jockey told me Danilo was in Africa then, in June, for a fortnight, which must have been just after he had stayed with Nerissa, because he talked about having seen her. After that, he presumably went back to the States for a while, but the horses went on losing, so obviously he was not doing the actual stopping himself. It's difficult to see how he could ever have had the opportunity of doing it himself, anyway, but he seems to have an understanding with Arknold's head lad; and I'll admit that all I have to go on *there* is the way they look at each other. Danilo never guards his face, by the way. He guards his tongue, but not his face. So suppose it is Barty, the head boy, who is arranging the actual fixing, with suitable rewards from Danilo."

"Well—if you are right—how?"

"There are only two completely undetectable ways which can go on safely for a long time: overexercising, which loses the race on the gallops at home (though in that case it is always the trainer who's guilty, and people notice and talk); and the way I think Barty must be using, the plain old simple bucket of water."

Charlie said, "Keep a horse thirsty, maybe even put lashings of salt in its feed, and then give it a bucket or two of water before the race?"

"Absolutely. The poor things can't last the distance with three or four gallons sloshing around in their stomachs. And as for Barty, even if he were not always around to supply the water at the right time, he has all the other lads intimidated to such an extent that they'd probably cut off their own ears if he told them to."

"But," she objected, "if the head lad has been doing this for weeks and weeks surely the trainer would have cottoned on?"

"I think he has," I agreed. "I don't think he likes it, but he's letting it pass. He said it was 'too much' when one of Nerissa's best colts got beaten out of sight yesterday in a poor class race. And then he himself gave me a version of what might be going on, and what may happen in the future. He accused me of implying that he was losing with the horses so that Nerissa would sell them; he would then buy them cheap, start winning, and sell them at a vast profit for stud. I had only vaguely been thinking along those lines, but he crystallized it as though the thought were by no means new to him. It was that, really, which set me wondering about Danilo. That, and the way he was smiling while he watched one of the horses go out to race. That smile was all wrong. Anyway, if he can reduce the value of the horses to nearly nil by Nerissa's death, there will be a great deal less duty to pay on them than if they were all winning. The difference would run into many thousands, considering there are eleven horses. That would be a profit well worth the outlay on a couple of trips to South Africa and payola for the head lad. I think they are going to change the system, but as the tax laws stand at present he would have to be in line for the residue of the estate for there to be any point in his doing it."

"Unscramble my brains," Charlie said.

I laughed. "Well. Estate duty will be paid on everything Nerissa owns. Then the separate bequests will be handed out. Then what is left will be the residue. Even though the horses are in South Africa, estate duty on them will be levied in England, because Nerissa lives there. So if the estate has to pay out all those thousands in death duties on the horses, there will be that many thousands less in the residue for Danilo to inherit."

"Gotcha," she said. "And wow again."

"Then, after they are safely his, he stops the watering lark, lets them win, sells them or puts them to stud, and collects some more lolly."

"Oh, neat. Very neat."

"Pretty simple, too."

"I say," she said, "isn't there anything we could try along the same lines? All that mountain of surtax we pay, and then when one of us dies we lose another terrific chunk of what we've paid tax on once already."

I smiled. "Can't think of anything which fluctuates in value so easily as a horse."

"Let's buy some more, then."

"And of course you have to know, pretty well to a month, exactly when you are going to die."

"Oh, damn it," Charlie said, laughing. "Life is a lot of little green apples and pains in the neck."

"I wonder if 'a pain in the neck' originated from the ax."

"The axman cometh," she said. "Or for ax, read tax."

"I'll bring you back a nugget or two from the gold mine," I promised.

"Oh, thanks."

"And I'll telephone again on—say, Thursday evening. I'll be down in the Kruger Park by then. Would Thursday be O.K. for you?"

"Yes," she said soberly, the fun vanishing like mist. "I'll go over to Nerissa's before then, and see what I can find out."

9

You can't keep a good Dakota down.

There were two of them waiting at the small Rand Airport near Germiston racecourse, sitting on their tail wheels and pointing their dolphin snouts hopefully to the sky.

We unloaded one of them at eight on Monday morning, along with several other passengers and a sizable amount of freight. Day and time were unkind to Roderick, making it clearer than ever that letting go of a semblance of youth was long overdue. The mature man, I reflected, was in danger of wasting altogether the period when he could look most impressive; if Roderick was not careful, he would slip straight from aging youth to obvious old age, a mistake more often found in show business than journalism.

He was wearing a brown long-sleeved suède jacket with fringes hanging from every possible edge. Under that, an open-necked shirt in an orange-tan color, trousers which were cut to prove masculinity, and the latest thing in desert boots.

Van Huren, at the other end of the scale in dark city suit, arrived last, took control easily, and shunted us all aboard. The Dakota trip took an hour, and landed a hundred and sixty miles south, at an isolated mining town which had "Welkom" on the mat and on practically everything else.

The van Huren mine was on the far side from the airport, and a small bus had come to fetch us. The town was neat, modern, geometrical, with straight bright rows of little square houses and acres of glass-walled supermarkets. A town of hygienic packaging, with its lifeblood deep underground.

Our destination looked at first sight to be a collection of huge whitish-gray tips, one with its railway track climbing to the top. Closer acquaintance revealed the wheel in scaffolding at the top of the shaft, masses of administration buildings and miners' hostels, and dozens of decorative date palms. The short frondy trees, their sunlit leaf branches chattering gently in the light breeze, did a fair job at beating the starkness, like gift wrapping on a shovel.

Van Huren apologized with a smile for not being able to go down the mine with us himself; he had meetings all morning which could not be switched.

"But we'll meet for lunch," he promised, "and for that drink which you will all need!"

The guide, someone a couple of rungs down the hierarchy had detailed to show us round, was a grumpy young Afrikaner who announced that he was Pieter Losenwoldt and a mining engineer, and more or less explicitly added that his present task was a nuisance, an interruption of his work, and beneath his dignity.

He showed us into a changing room where we were to sink all differences in white overalls, heavy boots, and high-domed helmets.

"Don't take anything of your own down the mine except your underpants and a handkerchief," he said dogmatically. "No cameras." He glowered at the equipment Conrad had lugged along. "Camera flashes are not safe. And no matches. No lighters. When I say nothing, I mean nothing."

"How about wallets?" Danilo demanded, antagonized and showing it.

Losenwoldt inspected him, saw a better-looking, richer, more obviously likable person than himself, and reacted with an even worse display of chips on shoulder.

"Leave everything," he said impatiently. "The room will be locked. Everything will be quite safe until you get back."

He went away while we changed, and came back in similar togs.

"Ready? Right. Now, we are going four thousand feet down. The lift descends at twenty-eight hundred feet a minute. It will be hot in places underground. Anyone who feels claustrophobic or ill in any way is to ask to return to the surface straight away. Understand?"

He got five nods and no affection.

He peered suddenly at me, speculating, then dismissed the thought with pursed lips and a shake of the head. No one enlightened him.

"Your light-packs are on the table. Please put them on."

The light-packs consisted of a flat power pack, which one wore slung over the lumbar region, and a light which clipped onto the front of the helmet. A lead led from one to the other. The power packs fastened round one's waist with webbing, and were noticeably heavy.

Much like the seven dwarfs, we tramped forth to the mine. The cage we went down in had half sides only, so that the realities of rock-burrowing hit at once. No comfort. A lot of noise. The nasty thought of all that space below one's booted feet.

It presumably took less than two minutes to complete the trip, but as I was jammed tight between Evan, whose hot eyes looked for once apprehensive, and a six-foot-four twenty-stone miner, who had joined with several cronies at the top, I couldn't exactly check it by stopwatch.

We landed with a clang at the bottom and disembarked. Another contingent were waiting to go up, and as soon as we were out, they loaded and operated the system of buzzers which got them clanking on their way.

"Get into the trucks," said Losenwoldt bossily. "They hold twelve people in each."

Conrad surveyed the two trucks, which looked like wire cages on wheels with accommodation for one large dog if he curled himself up, and said to me, "Sardines have struck for less."

I laughed. But the trucks did hold twelve; just. The last man in had to sit in the hole that did duty as doorway, and trust to what he could find to hang on to that he didn't fall out. Evan was last in. He hung on to Losenwoldt's overalls. Losenwoldt didn't like it.

Loaded to capacity, the trucks trundled off along the tunnel which stretched straight ahead for as far as one could see. The walls were painted white to about four feet; then there was a two-inch-deep bright red line, then above that the natural gray rock.

Conrad asked Losenwoldt why the red line was there; he had to shout to be heard, and he had to shout twice, as Losenwoldt was in no hurry to answer.

Finally he shouted back crossly, "It is a guide to the tunnelers. When the tunnel is painted like this, they can see that they are making it straight and level. The red line is an eyeline."

Conversation lapsed. The trucks covered about two miles at a fast trot and stopped abruptly at nowhere in particular. It was suddenly possible to hear oneself speak again, and Losenwoldt said, "We get out here and walk."

Everyone unsqueezed himself and climbed out. The miners strode purposefully away down the tunnel, but there was, it seemed, a set pattern for instructing visitors. Losenwoldt said ungraciously (but at least he said it), "Along the roof of the tunnel you can see the cables from which we have the electric lights." The lights were spaced overhead at regular intervals so that the whole tunnel was evenly lit. "Beside it there is a live electric rail." He pointed. "That provides power for the trucks which take the rock along to the surface. The rock goes up in a faster lift, at more than three thousand feet a minute. That big round pipe up there carries air. The mine is ventilated by blowing compressed air into it at many points."

We all looked at him like kids round a teacher, but he had come to the end of that bit of official spiel, so he turned his back on us and trudged away down the tunnel.

We followed.

We met a large party of black Africans walking the other way. They were dressed as we were, except that they were wearing jackets on top of their overalls.

Roderick asked, "Why the jackets?"

Losenwoldt said, "It is hot down here. The body gets accustomed. Without a jacket, it feels cold on reaching the surface. You can catch chills."

Evan nodded wisely. We went on walking.

Eventually we came to a wider space, where a second tunnel branched off to the right. Another party of Africans was collecting there, putting on jackets and being checked against a list.

"They have finished their shift," Losenwoldt said, in his clipped way, hating us. "They are being checked to make sure none of them is still underground when blasting takes place."

"Blasting, dear boy?" said Conrad vaguely.

The expert eyed him with disfavor. "The rock has to be blasted. One cannot remove it with pickaxes."

"But I thought this was a gold mine, dear boy. Surely one does not need blasting to remove gold? Surely one digs out gravel and sifts the gold from it."

Losenwoldt looked at him with near contempt. "In California and Alaska, and in some other places, this may be so. In South Africa, the gold is not visible. It is in minute particles in rock. One has to blast out the gold-bearing rock, take it to the surface, and put it through many processes to remove the gold. In this mine, one has to take three tons of rock to the surface to obtain one ounce of pure gold."

I think we were all struck dumb. Danilo's mouth actually dropped open.

"In some mines here in the Odendaalsrus gold field," Losenwoldt went on, seeming not to notice the stunned reaction, "it is necessary to remove only one and a half tons to get one ounce. Those mines are of course the richest. Some need more than this one: three and a half or four tons."

Roderick looked around him. "And all the gold has been taken from here? And from where we came?"

His turn for the look of pity-contempt.

"This tunnel is not made through gold-bearing rock. This tunnel is just to enable us to get to the gold-bearing rock, which is in this part of the mine. It can only be reached at more than four thousand feet underground."

"Good God," Conrad said, and spoke for us all.

Losenwoldt plodded grudgingly on with his lecture, but his audience was riveted.

"The reef—that is to say, the gold-bearing rock—is only a thin layer. It slopes underground from the north, being deepest beyond Welkom, further south. It extends for about eight miles from east to west, and about fourteen miles from north to south, but its limits are irregular. It is nowhere more than three feet in depth, and in this mine it is on average thirteen inches."

He collected a lot of truly astonished glances, but only Danilo had a question.

"I suppose it must be worth it," he said doubtfully. "All this work and equipment, just to get so little gold."

"It must be worth it or we would not be here," said Losenwoldt squelchingly, which I at least interpreted as ignorance of the profit and loss figures of the business. But it must be worth it, I reflected, or van Huren would not live in a sub-palace.

No one else said anything. Seldom had cheerful casual conversation been more actively discouraged. And Evan's natural inclination to put himself in charge of everything was being severely inhibited; in fact, after looking apprehensive in the lift he now seemed the most oppressed of us all at the thought of millions of tons of rock pressing down directly above our heads.

"Right," said Losenwoldt with heavy satisfaction at having reduced the ranks to pulped silence. "Now, switch on your helmet lights. There are no electric lights further along there." He pointed up the branch tunnel. "We will go to see the tunneling in progress."

He strode off without checking to see that we all followed, but we did, though Evan gave a backward glance in the direction of the shaft which would have warned a more careful guide not to take too much for granted.

The tunnel ran straight for a while and then curved to the right. As we approached the corner, we could hear a constantly increasing roaring noise, and round on the new tack it noticeably increased.

"What's that noise?" Evan asked in a voice still the safe side of active anxiety.

Losenwoldt said over his shoulder, "Partly the air conditioning, partly the drilling," and kept on going. The spaced electric light bulbs came to an end. The light on our helmets picked the way.

Suddenly, far ahead, we could discern a separate glimmer of light beyond the beams we were ourselves throwing. Closer contact divided the glimmer into three individual helmet lights pointing in the same direction as ours, but these lights lit only solid rock. We were coming to the end of the tunnel.

The walls at this point were no longer painted a comforting white with a red line, but became the uniform dark gray of the basic rock, which somehow emphasized the fanaticism of burrowing so deep in the earth's undisturbed crust, in search of invisible yellow dust.

The air pipe stopped abruptly, the compressed air roaring out from its open mouth. Beyond that, the noise of the drilling took over, as aggressive to the eardrums as six fortissimo discothèques.

There were three miners standing on a wooden platform, drilling a hole into the rock up near the eight-foot-high roof. Our lights shone on the sweat on their dark skins and reflected on the vests and thin trousers they wore in place of everyone else's thick white overalls.

The racket came from a compressor standing on the ground, as much as from the drill itself. We watched for a while. Evan tried to ask something, but it would have taken a lip reader to get anywhere.

Finally Losenwoldt, with tight mouth, jerked his head for us to go back. We followed him, glad about the lessening load on our ears. Walking last, I turned round where the air pipe ended, switched off my helmet light for a moment, and looked back. Three men on their scaffolding, intent on their task, enveloped in noise, and lit only by the glowworms on their heads. When I had turned and gone, they would be alone with the primeval darkness closing in behind them. I was left with a fanciful impression of a busy team of devils moling along toward Inferno.

Once back in the wider section, Losenwoldt continued our instruction.

"They were drilling holes about six feet deep, with tungsten drills. That"—he pointed—"is a pile of drills."

We looked where he pointed. The horizontal stack of six-foot rods by the tunnel wall had looked more like a heap of unused piping before; but they were solid metal rods about two inches in diameter with a blade of tungsten shining at the end of each.

"The rods have to be taken to the surface every day, to be sharpened."

We nodded like wise owls.

"Those three men have nearly finished drilling for today. They have drilled many holes in the face of the tunnel. Each hole will receive its charge of explosive, and after the blasting the broken rock will be removed. Then the drillers return and start the process again."

"How much tunnel can you make in one day?" Roderick asked.

"Eight feet a shift."

Evan leaned against the rock wall and passed a hand over a forehead that Clifford Wenkins could not have bettered.

"Don't you ever use pitprops?" he said.

Losenwoldt answered the face of the question and didn't see the fear behind it.

"Of course not. We are tunneling not through earth but through bedrock. There is no danger of the tunnel collapsing inward. Occasionally, loosened slabs of rock fall from the roof or the wall. This usually happens in areas recently blasted. Where we see such loosened rocks, we pull them down, if we can, so that there is no danger of them falling on anyone later."

Evan failed to look comforted. He dug out his handkerchief and mopped up.

"What sort of explosive do you use for blasting?" Danilo asked.

Losenwoldt still didn't like him, and didn't answer. Roderick, who was also interested, repeated the same question.

Losenwoldt ostentatiously stifled a sigh and replied in more staccato sentences than ever. "It is dynagel. It is a black powder. It is kept in locked red boxes fastened to the tunnel wall."

He pointed to one of them a little farther on. I had walked past two or three of them, padlocks and all, without wondering what they were for.

Danilo, with sarcasm, said to Roderick, "Ask him what happens when they blast," and Roderick did.

Losenwoldt shrugged. "What would you expect? But no one sees the blasting. Everyone is out of the mine before the charges are detonated. No one returns down the mine for four hours after blasting."

"Why not, dear boy?" drawled Conrad.

"Dust," Losenwoldt said succinctly.

"When do we get to see this gold rock—this reef?" asked Danilo.

"Now." Losenwoldt pointed along the continuation of the main tunnel. "Further down there, it will be very hot. There is a stretch with no air conditioning. Beyond that, there is air again. Leave your helmet lights on; you will need them. Take care where you walk. The floor of the tunnel is rough in places."

He finished with a snap and, as before, set off with his back to us.

Again we followed.

I said to Evan, "Are you O.K.?" which irritated him into straightening his spine and saying of course he damn well was—did I think he was a fool?

"No," I said.

"Right, then." He strode purposefully past me to get nearer to the pearls spat from Losenwoldt's lips, and I again brought up the rear.

The heat farther on was intense but dry, so that although one felt it, it produced no feeling of sweat. The tunnel at this point grew rough, with uneven walls, no painted lines, no lights, and a broken-up floor; it also sloped gradually downhill. We trudged on, boots crunching on the gritty surface.

The farther we went, the more activity we came across. Men in white overalls were everywhere, busy, carrying equipment, with their helmet lights shining on other people's concentrated faces. The peak of the helmets tended to throw a dark band of shadow across each man's eyes, and once or twice I had to touch Roderick, who was in front of me, so that he would turn and reassure me that I was still following the right man.

At the end of the hot stretch, it felt like stepping straight into the Arctic. Losenwoldt stopped there and consulted briefly with two other young miners he found talking to each other.

"We will split up here," he said finally. "You two with me." He pointed to Roderick and Evan. "You two with Mr. Anders." He assigned Conrad and Danilo to a larger version of himself. "You"—he pointed at me—"with Mr. Yates."

Yates, younger than the others, appeared unhelpfully subservient to them, and spoke with a slight speech impediment on the order of a cleft palate. He gave me a twitchy smile and said he hoped I wouldn't mind, he wasn't used to showing people round, it wasn't usually his job.

"It's kind of you to do so," I said soothingly.

The others were moving off in their little groups and were soon lost in the general crowd of white overalls.

"Come along, then."

We continued down the tunnel. I asked my new guide what the gradient was.

"About one in twenty," he said. But after that he lapsed into silence, and I reckoned if I wanted to know any more I would have to ask. Yates did not know the conducted-tour script like Losenwoldt, who in retrospect did not seem too bad.

Holes appeared from time to time in the left-hand wall, with apparently a big emptiness behind them.

"I thought this tunnel was through solid rock," I observed. "So what are those holes?"

"Oh . . . we are now in the reef. The reef has been removed from much of that portion behind the wall. In a minute, I'll be able to show you better."

"Does the reef slope at one in twenty, then?" I asked.

He thought it a surprising question. "Of course," he said.

"That tunnel which is still being drilled, back there, where is that going?"

"To reach another area of reef."

Yes. Silly question. The reef spread literally for miles. Quite. Removing the reef must be rather like chipping a thin slice of ham out of a thick bread sandwich.

"What happens when all the reef is removed?" I asked. "There must be enormous areas with nothing holding up the layers of rock above."

He answered willingly enough. "We do not remove all supports. For instance, the wall of the tunnel is thick, despite the holes, which are for blasting and ventilation purposes. It will hold the roof up in all this area. Eventually, of course, when this tunnel is worked out and disused, the layers will gradually close together. I believe that most of Johannesburg sank about three feet, as the layers below it closed together, after all the reef was out."

"Not recently?" I said, surprised.

"Oh, no. Long ago. The Rand gold fields are shallower and mining began there first."

People were carrying tungsten rods up the tunnel and others were passing us going down it.

"We are getting ready to blast," Yates said. "All the drilling is finished and the engineers are setting the charges."

"We haven't very long, then," I said.

"Probably not."

"I'd like to see how they actually work the reef."

"Oh . . . yes. Just down here a bit further, then. I will take you to the nearest part. There are others further down."

We came to a larger than usual hole in the wall. It stretched from the floor to above five feet up, but one could not walk straight through it, as it sloped sharply upward inside.

He said, "You will have to mind your head. It is very shallow in here."

"O.K.," I said.

He gestured to me to crawl in ahead of him, which I did. The space was about three feet high but extended out of sight in two directions. A good deal of ham had already gone from this part of the sandwich.

Instead of a firm rock floor, we were now scrambling over a bed of sharp-edged chips of rock, which rattled away as we tried to climb up over them. I went some way into the flat cavern and then waited for Yates. He was close behind, looking across to our right where several men lower down were working along a curving thirty-foot stretch of the far wall.

"They are making final checks on the explosive charges," he said. "Soon everyone will begin to leave."

"This loose stuff we are lying on," I said. "Is this the reef?"

"Oh . . . no, not exactly. These are just chips of rock. See, the reef used to lie about midway up the stope."

"What is the stope?"

"Sorry. The stope is what we are now in. The place we take the reef from."

"Well, down there, in the part which is not blasted yet, how do you tell which is the reef?"

The whole thing looked the same to me. Dark gray from top to bottom. Dark gray uneven roof curving down in dark gray uneven walls, merging into dark gray shingle floor.

"I'll get you a piece," he said obligingly, and crawled on his stomach over to where his colleagues were working. It was barely possible to sit up in the stope. Just about possible to rise to hands and knees, if one kept one's head down. I supported myself on one elbow and watched him borrow a small hand pick and lever a sliver of rock out of the far wall.

He scrambled back.

"There you are. This is a piece of reef."

We focused both our lights on it. A two-inch-long gray sharp-edged lump with darker gray, slightly light-reflecting spots and streaks on its surface.

"What are those dark spots?" I said.

"That's the ore," he said. "The paler part is just ordinary rock. The more of those dark bits there are in the reef, the better the yield of gold per ton of rock."

"Then is this dark stuff gold?" I asked dubiously.

"It has gold in it," he said, nodding. "Actually it is made up of four elements: gold, silver, uranium, and chrome. When the reef is milled and treated, they are separated out. There is more gold than silver or uranium."

"Can I keep this piece?" I asked.

"Certainly." He cleared his throat. "I am sorry, but they have a job for me to do down there. Could you possibly find your own way back up the tunnel? You cannot get lost."

"That's all right," I said. "You go on. I don't want to interfere with your job."

"Thank you," he said, and scrambled away in haste to please the people who really mattered to him.

I stayed where I was for a while, watching the engineers and peering into the interminable dug-out space uphill. The light of my helmet couldn't reach its limits; it stretched away into impenetrable blackness.

The workers below me were thinning out, returning to the tunnel to make their way back toward the shaft. I put the tiny piece of reef in my pocket, took a last look round, and began to inch my way back to the hole where I had come in. I turned round to go into the tunnel feet first, but as I started to shuffle backward I heard someone climbing into the stope behind me, the light from his helmet flashing on my overalls. I stopped to let him go by. He made a little forward progress, and I glanced briefly over my shoulder to see who it was. I could see only the peak of his helmet, and shadow beneath.

Then my own helmet tipped off forward and a large chunk of old Africa clobbered me forcefully on the back of the head.

Stunned, I seemed to feel consciousness ebb away slowly; I fell dizzily down endless mine shafts, with flashing dots before my eyes.

I had blacked out completely long before I hit the bottom.

10

Blackness.

Nothing.

I opened my eyes. Couldn't see. Put my hand to my face to feel if my eyelids were open.

They were.

Thought was entirely disconnected. I didn't know where I was, or why I was there, or why I couldn't see. Time seemed suspended. I couldn't decide whether I was asleep or not, and for a while I couldn't remember my own name.

Drifted away again. Came back. Snapped suddenly into consciousness. Knew I was awake. Knew I was me.

Still couldn't see.

I moved; tried to sit up. Discovered I was lying on my side. When I moved, I heard the crunching noise and felt the sharp rock chips shifting against my pressure.

In the stope.

Cautiously I put up a hand. The rock ceiling was a couple of feet above my head.

No helmet on my head. A tender lump on the back of it and a thumping pain inside it.

Bloody hell, I thought. I must have bashed my head. I'm in the stope. I can't see because there isn't any light. Everyone has left the mine. And the blasting charges will go off at any minute.

For a paralyzing age, I couldn't think beyond the fact that I was going to be blown to bits before I had even finished realizing it. After that I thought it might have been better if I'd been blown to bits before I woke up. At least I wouldn't now be awake and worrying. After that, and not before time, I began wondering what to do.

Light, first.

I felt around to my back, found the lead from the power pack, and gently pulled it. The other end scraped toward me over the choppy shingle, but when I picked up the torch I knew I wasn't going to get any light. The glass and the bulb were both smashed.

The light unit had come off the bracket of the helmet. I felt around with an outstretched hand but couldn't find the helmet.

Must get out, I thought urgently, and in the same split second wondered which way was out.

I made myself stay still. The last thing I remembered was agreeing with Yates that I could find my own way back. I must have been stupid enough to try to raise my head too high. Must literally have hit the roof. I couldn't remember doing it. The only thing that seemed clear was that I had smashed my helmet light when I fell, and that no one had seen me lying there in the dark.

Bloody fool, I cursed myself. Clumsy bloody fool, getting into this mess.

Gingerly, with one arm outstretched, I shifted myself a foot forward. My fingers found nothing to touch except stone chips.

I had to know which way I was going. Otherwise, I thought, I may be crawling away from safety, not toward it. I had to find the hole into the tunnel.

I picked up a handful of the flinty pebbles and began throwing them methodically round in a circle, starting on my right. It was an erratic process, as some hit the roof and some the ground, but a few went far enough before they fell to assure me that there was a space all around me in front.

I rolled over on my back and the power pack dug into me. I unfastened the webbing and pulled it off. Then I threw another handful of stones in an arc round my legs.

The wall of the tunnel was there. A lot of the stones hit it.

My heart by then was thudding so much it was deafening me. Shut up, shut up, I said to myself. Don't be so bloody scared; it isn't of any practical use.

I threw more stones, this time not to find the wall, but the hole in it. I found it almost at once. Threw more stones to make sure; but there it had to be, just to the left of where my feet were pointing, because all the stones that I threw there were falling farther away, and clattering after they landed. They weren't round enough to roll, but heavy enough to continue downhill when they fell. Downhill . . . on the steep little slope from the stope into the tunnel.

More stones. I moved my feet, then my whole body, until the hole was straight in front over my toes. Then on my elbows and my bottom, keeping my head well back, I shuffled forward.

More stones. Hole still there.

More shuffling. Another check.

It couldn't have been more than ten feet. Felt like ten miles.

I tentatively swept my arms around in the air. Could feel the roof, nothing else.

Went forward another two or three feet. Felt around with my arms. Touched solid rock. Ahead, to the right.

Another foot forward. Felt my feet turn abruptly downward, bending my knees. Put both my hands out sidewise and forward and felt rock on both sides. Halfway out of the hole . . . and carefully, lying flat, I inched forward until my feet scrunched on the tunnel floor. Even then, I bent my knees and continued slithering without raising my head, all too aware of the hard sharpness of the rock above and the vulnerability of my unhelmeted skull.

I ended on my knees in the tunnel, gasping and feeling as frightened as ever.

Think.

The holes had been in the left-hand wall as we came down. Once in the tunnel, Yates had said, I couldn't get lost.

O.K. Turn right. Straight forward. Dead simple.

I stood up carefully, and with the hole at my back, turned right. Put my hand on the rough rock wall. Took a step forward.

The scrunch of my boot on the rock floor made me realize for the first time how quiet it was. In the stope, I had had both the stones and my own heart to fill my ears. Now there was nothing. The silence was as absolute as the darkness.

I didn't waste time brooding about it. Moved ahead as fast as I dared, step by careful step. No sound. That meant the air conditioning had been switched off, which hardly mattered; there was a mineful still to breathe, even if it was hot.

My hand lost the wall suddenly, and my heart set up a fresh chorus. Taking a grip on my breath, I moved a step backward. Right hand back on wall. O.K. Breathe out. Now, kneel down, grope along floor, keep in contact with wall on right. Navigate past another of the holes which led through to the stope.

Holes which would let the blast out of the stope when the charges exploded.

Blast traveled far when confined in a long narrow space. Blast was a killing force, as deadly as flying rocks.

Oh, God, I thought. Oh, hell's bloody bells. What did one think about if one was probably going to die at any minute?

I thought about getting as far back up the mine as quickly as I could. I thought about not losing contact with the right-hand wall when I passed the holes in it, because if I did I might turn round in the darkness and find the other wall instead, and go straight back toward the explosion. I didn't think about anything else at all. Not even about Charlie.

I went on. The air became hotter and hotter. The stretch that had been hot coming down was now an assault on the nerve endings.

Struggling on, I couldn't tell how fast I was going. Very slowly, I imagined. Like in a nightmare, trying to flee from a terror at one's heels and not being able to run.

I got back in the end to the wider space, and the explosion still hadn't happened. Another explosion was due to take place down the branch tunnel also, but the bend in the tunnel should disperse some of the blast.

Beginning at last to let hope creep in, and keeping my hand on the right-hand wall literally for dear life, I trudged slowly on. Two miles to go, maybe, to the bottom of the shaft . . . but every step taking me nearer to safety.

Those lethal pockets of dynagel never did explode; or not while I was down the mine.

One minute, I was taking another step into darkness. The next, I was blinded by light.

I shut my eyes, wincing against the brightness, and I stopped walking and leaned against the wall instead. When I opened my eyes again, the electric lights were blazing in all their glory, and the tunnel looked as solid, safe, and reassuringly painted as it had done on the way in.

Weakened by relief, I shifted off the wall and went on again, with knees that were suddenly trembling and a head that was back to aching like a hangover.

There was a background hum now again in the mine, and from far away up the tunnel a separate noise detached itself and grew louder: the rattle of the wire cage trucks making the outward journey.

Eventually it stopped and then there was the sound of several boots, and then finally, round a shallow curve, came four men in white overalls.

Hurrying.

They spotted me, and began to run. Slowed and stopped

just before they reached me, with relief that I was mobile showing on their faces. Losenwoldt was one of them; I didn't know the others.

"Mr. Lincoln, are you all right?" one of them asked anxiously.

"Sure," I said. It didn't sound right. I said it again. "Sure." Much better.

"How did you get left behind?" Losenwoldt said reprovingly, shifting all possible blame from himself. Not that I would have allotted him any; he was just forestalling it.

I said, "I'm sorry to have been such a nuisance. . . . I think I must have hit my head and knocked myself out, but I can't actually remember how." I wrinkled my forehead. "So damned stupid of me."

One of them said, "Where were you, exactly?"

"In the stope," I said.

"Good grief. . . . You probably lifted your head too sharply, or maybe a piece of rock fell from the roof and caught you."

"Yes," I said.

Another of them said, "If you were unconscious in the stope, however did you get back here?"

I told them about the stones. They didn't say anything. Just looked at each other.

One of them walked round my back and after a moment said, "There's some blood on your hair and down your neck, but it looks dry. I don't think you're still bleeding." He came round to my side. "Do you feel all right to walk to the trucks? We brought a stretcher—just in case."

I smiled. "Guess I can walk."

We walked. I asked, "How did you discover I was down here?"

One of them said ruefully, "Our system of checking everyone is out of the mine before blasting is supposed to be infallible. And so it is, as far as the miners are concerned. But visitors . . . You see, we don't often have small groups of unofficial visitors, like today. Mr. van Huren seldom invites anyone, and no one else is allowed to. Nearly all the visitors we have here are official tourist groups, of about twenty people, and the mine more or less stops while we show them round, but we only do that every six weeks or so. We don't usually blast at all on those days. Today, though, one of your party felt ill and went back before the others, and I think everyone took it for granted that you had gone with him. Tim Yates said when he last saw you, you were just about to return up the tunnel."

"Yes," I said. "I remember that."

"The other three visitors went up together, and the checkers accounted for every miner, so we assumed everyone was out, and were all set to detonate . . ."

A tall thin man took up the story. "Then one of the men who counts the numbers going up and down in the lift said that one more had gone down than had come up. The shift checkers said it was impossible; each group had been checked out by name. The liftman said he was sure. Well, that only left the visitors. So we checked them. The three in the changing room said you hadn't changed yet, your clothes were still there, so you must be in the first-aid room with the one called Conrad, who had not felt well."

"Conrad," I exclaimed. I had thought they meant Evan. "What was wrong with him?"

"I think they said he had an attack of asthma. Anyway, we went and asked him, and he said you hadn't come up with him."

"Oh," I said blankly. Certainly if I had been with him I would have gone up, but I hadn't seen him at all after we had separated at the beginning of the reef.

We came to the trucks and climbed in. A lot of space with only five people instead of twelve.

"The one who was ill," Losenwoldt stated virtuously, "the stout one with the droopy mustache, he was not with me. If he had been, of course I would have escorted him back to the trucks, and of course I would have known you were not with him."

"Of course," I said dryly.

We clattered back along the tunnel to the bottom of the shaft, and from there, after the exchange of signal buzzes, rose in the cage through three-quarters of a mile of rock up to the sunlight. Its brilliance was momentarily painful, and it was also cold enough to start me shivering.

"Jacket," exclaimed one of my escorts. "We took down a blanket—should have put it around you." He hurried off into a small building by the shaft and came back with a much-used tweed sports coat, which he held for me to put on.

There was an anxious-looking reception committee hovering around: Evan, Roderick, Danilo, and van Huren himself.

"My dear fellow," he said, peering at me as if to reassure himself that I was real. "What can I say?"

"For heaven's sake," I said, "it was my own fault and I'm terribly sorry to have caused all this fuss." Van Huren looked relieved and smiled, so did Evan, Roderick, and Danilo. I turned back to the three strangers who had come down for me; Losenwoldt had already gone. "Thank you," I said. "Thank you very much."

They all grinned. "We want payment," one said.

I must have looked bewildered. I was wondering what was right. How much.

"Your autograph," one of them explained.

"Oh." I laughed. "O.K."

One of them produced a notebook, and I wrote a thank-you to each of them, on three separate pages. And cheap at the price, I thought.

The mine doctor swabbed stone dust from the cut on my head, said it wasn't deep, nothing serious, didn't need stitching, didn't need a plaster, even, unless I wanted one.

"I don't," I said.

"Good, good. Swallow these, then. In case you develop a headache."

I swallowed obediently. Collected Conrad, now breathing normally again, from a rest room next door, and followed directions to the bar and dining room for lunch. On the way, we swapped operations, so to speak. Neither of us felt much pleased with himself.

The five of us sat at a table with Quentin van Huren, plus two other senior executives whose names I never learned. My narrow escape was chewed over by everyone all over again, and I said with feeling to Roderick that I would be much obliged if he would keep my embarrassment out of his inky columns.

He grinned. "Yeah. . . . Much better copy if you'd been blown up. Not much news value in a checker doing his job properly."

"Thank God for that," I said.

Conrad looked at me. "There must be a jinx on you in South Africa, dear boy. That's the second time you've been close to extinction within a week."

I shook my head. "No jinx. Just the opposite. I've survived twice. Look at it that way."

"Only seven lives left," Conrad said.

The talk worked back to gold. I suspected that in Welkom it always did, like Newmarket and horses.

"Say, how do you get it out of the rock?" Danilo demanded. "You can't even see it."

Van Huren smiled indulgently. "Danilo, it is simple. You crush the rock in mills until it is powdered. You add cyanide of potassium, which holds the gold particles in solution. You add zinc, to which the gold particles stick. You then wash out the acid. You then separate the zinc from the gold again, using aqua regia, and finally you retrieve the gold."

"Oh, simple," Conrad agreed. "Dear boy."

Van Huren warmed to him, and smiled with pleasure. "That is not exactly all. One still has to refine the gold— to remove impurities by melting it to white heat in giant crucibles, and pouring it out into bricks. The residue flows away, and you are left with the pure gold."

Danilo did a rapid calculation. "You'll have gotten around three thousand five hundred tons of reef out of the mine, for one little old brick."

"That's so," agreed van Huren, smiling. "Give or take a ton or two."

"How much do you bring out in a week?" Danilo asked.

"Just over forty thousand metric tons."

Danilo's eyes flickered as he did the mental arithmetic. "That means . . . er . . . about eleven and a half gold bricks every week."

"Do you want a job in the accounting department, Danilo?" asked van Huren, much amused.

But Danilo hadn't finished. "Each brick weighs seventy-two pounds, right? So that makes . . . let's see . . . around eight hundred pounds of gold a week. Say, what's the price of gold per ounce? Gee, this is sure the right business to be in. What a gas!" He was deeply stimulated, as he had been by the whole trip, with a strong inner excitement shining out of his eyes. An attraction toward moneymaking, and the calculations needed to work out estate-duty dodging, seemed to me to be all of a piece.

Van Huren, still smiling, said, "You're forgetting the wages, the maintenance, and the shareholders. There are only a few grains of dust left after they've all taken their cut."

Danilo's curving mouth showed he didn't believe it. Roderick shot an orange cuff out of the brown suède sleeve to reveal half a ton of tiger's-eye doing duty as a cuff link.

"Don't you own the mine altogether, then, Quentin?" he asked.

The executives and van Huren himself smiled indulgently at Roderick for his naïveté.

"No," van Huren said. "My family own the land and the mineral rights. Technically, I suppose, we do own the gold. But it takes an enormous amount of capital, many millions of rands, to sink a shaft and build all the surface plant needed. About twenty-five years ago, my brother and I floated a company to raise capital to start drilling, so the company has hundreds of private shareholders."

"That mine doesn't look twenty-five years old," I objected amiably.

Van Huren shifted his smiling eyes in my direction and went on explaining.

"The part you saw this morning is the newest tunnel, and the deepest. There are other tunnels at higher levels. In past years, we have taken out all the upslope areas of the reef."

"And there's still a lot left?"

Van Huren's smile had the ease of one who would never be short of a thousand. "It will see Jonathan out," he said.

Evan chose to find the mechanics and economics less interesting than the purpose, and waved his arms about as he pinned every gaze down in turn with his fierce eyes and declaimed with his usual intensity.

"What is gold for, though? This is what we should be asking. What everyone should be asking. What is the *point?* Everyone goes to so much trouble to get it, and pays so much for it, and it has no real *use.*"

"Gold-plated lunar bugs," I murmured.

Evan glared at me. "Everyone digs it out of the ground here and puts it back underground at Fort Knox, where it never sees daylight again. . . . Don't you see—the whole thing is *artificial?* Why should the whole world's wealth be based on a yellow metal which has no *use?*"

"Good for filling teeth," I said conversationally.

"And for pure radio contacts in transistor units," Roderick added, joining the game.

Van Huren listened and watched as if he found the entertainment a nice change for a Monday. I stopped baiting Evan, though, because after seeing the mine I half held his views.

I traveled back to Johannesburg in the Dakota that evening, sitting next to Roderick and feeling a trifle worn. A hot afternoon spent walking round the surface buildings of the mine, watching gold being poured from a crucible, seeing (and hearing) the ore being crushed, and visiting one of the miners' hostels had done no good at all to a throbbing head. Half a dozen times, I had almost dropped out, but—especially with Roderick's ready typewriter in the background—I hadn't wanted to make a fuss.

The visit to the hostel had been best; lunch was being cooked for the next surface shift off work, and we tasted it in the kitchen. Vast vats of thick broth with a splendid flavor, vegetables I couldn't identify and hadn't the energy to ask about, and thick wads of cream-colored mealie bread, a sort of fatless version of pastry.

From there we went next door into the hostel's bar, where the first of the returning shift were settling down to the serious business of drinking what looked like half-gallon plastic tubs of milky cocoa.

"That's Bantu beer," said our afternoon guide, who had proved as sweet as Losenwoldt was sour.

We drank some. It had a pleasant dry flavor but tasted nothing like beer.

"Is it alcoholic, dear boy?" Conrad asked.

The dear boy said it was, but weak. Considering that we saw one man dispatch his whole tubful in two great draughts, the weakness was just as well.

Our guide beckoned to one of the men sitting at a table with his colleagues, and he got to his feet and came over. He was tall and not young, and he had a wide white grin which I found infectious.

The guide said, "This is Piano Nyembezi. He is the checker who insisted we had left someone down the mine."

"Was it you?" I asked with interest.

"*Yebo,*" he said, which I later learned meant "yes" in Zulu. ("No" turned out to consist of a click, a glottal stop, and an "aa" sound. As far as a European was concerned, it was impossible to say no in a hurry.)

"Well, Piano," I said. "Thank you very much." I put out my hand and he shook it, an event which drew large smiles from his friends, an indrawn breath from our guide, a shake of the head from Roderick, and no reaction whatsoever from Evan, Conrad, or Danilo.

There was a certain amount of scuffling in the background, and then one of the others brought forward a well-thumbed copy of a film magazine.

"It is Piano's paper," the newcomer said, and thrust it into his hands. Nyembezi looked embarrassed, but showed me what it was. Full page, and as boring-looking as usual.

Wrinkling my nose, I took the magazine from him and wrote across the bottom of my picture, "I owe my life to Piano Nyembezi," and signed my name.

"He'll keep that forever," the guide said.

Until tomorrow, perhaps, I thought.

The Dakota droned on. The evening sun fell heavily across my eyelids as we banked round onto a new course, and I cautiously lifted my head off the seat back and put it down the other way. The cut on my head, though not deep, was sore.

For some reason, the small movement triggered off a few sleepy nerve cells, and in a quiet fashion I remembered that there had been someone with me in the stope.

I remembered I had been turning round to leave feet first, and had stopped to let someone else in. I remembered that I hadn't seen his face, didn't know who he was.

If he had been there when I bashed my head, why on earth hadn't he helped me?

Such was my fuzzy state of mind that it took me a whole minute more to move on to the conclusion that he hadn't helped me because he'd applied the rock himself.

I opened my eyes with a jolt. Roderick's face was turned toward mine. I opened my mouth to tell him. Then I shut it again, firmly. I did not in the least want to tell the Rand *Daily Star*.

11

I used a lot of the time I could more profitably have spent sleeping that night in coming to terms with the thought that someone might have tried to kill me.

Didn't know who. Couldn't guess why. And still was not certain whether my memory was complete; perhaps the other man in the stope had gone away again, and I had forgotten it.

Also, even if I had been a hundred percent certain, I didn't know what I should do about it.

Telephone van Huren? Start an investigation? But there had been so many people down the mine, all dressed alike, and half in darkness. Any investigation was going to produce more talk and doubt than results, and "Lincoln complains of attempted murder" was a gossip-column snippet I could do without.

Twice within a week I'd been close to extinction, Conrad had said.

It didn't make sense. It was only in films that the chaps I played got threatened and attacked, and made miraculous escapes.

Yet if I did nothing about it, what then? If someone

really had been trying to kill me, there was nothing to stop him trying again. How could I possibly protect myself every minute of every day—especially against unforeseen things like microphones and rocks in gold mines?

If—and I wasn't altogether convinced—two murder attempts had been made, they had both been arranged to look like accidents. So it was of little use taking future precautions against things like poison and bullets and knives in the back down dark alleys. One would have to beware instead of cars with no brakes, deadly insects in one's shoes, and disintegrating balconies.

I shied away for a long time from thinking about *who,* for it had to be someone who had been down in the mine.

A miner who didn't like my films taking steps to avoid sitting through any others? He wouldn't have to kill me; he could simply vote with his feet.

Someone smoldering from ungovernable professional jealousy? The only person I knew of who regularly swore undying hatred was Drix Goddart, but he was not yet in South Africa, let alone four thousand feet under Welkom.

None of the people working in the mine had known I was going to be there, and before the incident none of them had used my name.

That left . . . Oh, hell, I thought. Well, it left Evan . . . and Conrad . . . and Danilo . . . and Roderick. And also van Huren, who owned a lot of souls and could have things done by proxy.

As for *why,* Evan's professional resentment was surely not obsessive enough, and Danilo didn't know my guess of what he was up to with the horses; and in any case, even if he did, he wouldn't try to cover up such a minor crime with murder. More likely to confess and laugh, I would have thought, and meet a warning-off with a what-the-hell shrug.

Motives for Conrad, Roderick, and van Huren took even less cogitation. I couldn't rake up a decent one among them.

They had all (except Conrad, who had been in the surgery) looked relieved when I stepped safely out of the mine. Could they possibly have looked relieved just because I said I couldn't remember how I got knocked out?

It all seemed so improbable. I couldn't imagine any of them plotting away in murky labyrinths of villainy. It didn't make sense. I must, I concluded, be imagining things. I had been involved in too much fiction, and I had begun to project it onto reality.

I sighed. Realized that my head had stopped aching and that the unsettled feeling of concussion was subsiding, and presently went to sleep.

In the morning, the night thoughts seemed even more preposterous. It was Conrad who had suggested a connection between the mike and the mine; and Conrad had got it wrong.

Roderick telephoned at breakfast time. Would I care to have dinner at his flat, with Katya, just the three of us and no fuss? And when I hesitated for a few seconds over replying, he added quickly that it would all be strictly off the record; anything I said would not be taken down and used against me.

"O.K.," I agreed, with a smile in my voice and reservations in my mind. "Where do I find you?"

He told me the address, and said, "That chauffeur of yours will know where to find it."

"Oh. Yes," I said.

I put the receiver down slowly; but there was no reason why he shouldn't know about the hired car and driver, and there was of course his "source" at the Iguana. Roderick had all along known where I was going, what I was doing, and how often I brushed my teeth.

Almost before I had taken my hand off it, the telephone rang again.

Clifford Wenkins. Could he, er, that was to say, would it be convenient for him to come to the Club that morning to discuss, er, details, for the, er, première?

Er, yes, I said.

After that, Conrad rang. Was I going to travel down to the Kruger Park with him and Evan?

"How long are you staying there?" I asked.

"About ten days, I should think."

"No, then. I'll have to come back by next Tuesday, at the latest. I'll drive down separately. It will be better anyway to have two cars, with you and Evan concentrating on locations."

"Yeah," he said, sounding rather glad; he hadn't wanted to spend a week at close quarters keeping Evan and me off each other's throats, I imagined.

They would come around for a drink before lunch, he said. Evan, it appeared, was bursting with inspirations for his new film. (When was he not?)

After that, Arknold.

"Look, Mr. Lincoln. About Mrs. Cavesey's horses ... Look . . ." He petered heavily out.

After waiting in vain for him to start up again, I said, "I'll be here all morning, if you'd care to come over."

Three heavy breaths. Then he said, "Perhaps. Might be as well. Yes. All right. About eleven, then, after I've watched the horses work."

"See you," I said.

Hot sunshine, blue sky.

I went downstairs and drank my coffee out on the terrace, and read the newspapers. Close columns filled with local issues, all assuming a background of common knowledge which I didn't have. Reading them was like going into a film halfway through.

A man had been murdered in Johannesburg: found two days ago, with a wire twisted round his neck.

With a shiver, I put down the paper. No one was trying to murder me. I had decided it was nonsense. Another man's death had no business to be raising hairs on my skin. The trouble was, no one had told my subconscious that we were all through with red alerts.

"Morning," said a fresh young voice in my ear. "What are you doing?"

"Watching the flowers grow."

She sat down opposite me, grinning all over her fif-teen-year-old face.

"I've come to play tennis."

She wore a short white dress, white socks, white tennis shoes, and carried two rackets in zipped waterproof cov-ers. Her dark shoulder-length hair was held back by a green headband, and the van Huren wealth spoke as elo-quently as ever in her natural confidence and poise.

"Coffee?" I suggested.

"Rather have orange juice."

I ordered it.

"Didn't you just love the gold mine?" she demanded.

"I just did," I agreed, imitating Danilo's accent, as she had done his turn of phrase.

She wrinkled her nose, amused. "You never miss a damn thing, do you? Dad says you have an intuitive mind, whatever the hell that is."

"It means I jump to conclusions," I said.

She shook her head dubiously. "Uh-uh. He seemed to think it was good."

The orange juice came and she drank some, clanking the ice. She had long dark eyelashes and skin that was more cream than peaches. I stifled as always the inner lurch of regret that young girls like Sally gave me: my own daughter might grow up as pretty, but the zest and the flash would be missing.

She put down the glass and her eyes searched the Club buildings behind me.

"Have you seen Danilo anywhere?" she asked. "The swine said he'd be here at ten, and it's a quarter after al-ready."

"He was busy doing sums all yesterday," I said gravely. "I expect they wore him out."

"What sums?" she said suspiciously.

I told her.

She laughed. "He can't help doing sums, then, I shouldn't think. All Saturday at the races, he was doing it. A living computer, I called him." She took another orange sip. "I say, did you know he's a terrific gambler? He had ten rand on one of those horses. *Ten rand!*"

I thought van Huren had made a sensible job of her, if a ten-rand bet still seemed excessive.

"Mind you," she added. "The horse won. I went with him to collect the winnings. Twenty-five rand, would you believe it? He says he often wins. He was all sort of gay and laughing about it."

"Everyone loses in the end," I said.

"Oh, don't be such a downpour," she exploded. "Just like Dad."

Her eyes suddenly opened wider, and she transferred her attention to somewhere behind me.

Danilo joined us. White shorts, sturdy sunburned legs, light blue wind-cheater hanging open.

"Hi," he said happily, including us both.

"Hi," echoed Sally, looking smitten.

She left me and the half-finished orange juice without a backward glance, and went off with the bright boy as girls have been going off since Eve. But this girl's father had a gold mine; and Danilo had done his sums.

Arknold came, and the reception desk directed him to the garden. He shook hands, sat down, huffed and puffed, and agreed to a beer. Away in the distance, Danilo and Sally belted the ball sporadically over the net and laughed a lot in between.

Arknold followed my gaze, recognized Danilo, and consolidated his indecision in a heavy frown.

"I didn't know Danilo would be here," he said.

"He can't hear you."

"No—but— Look, Mister, do you mind if we go indoors?"

"If you like," I said; so we transferred to the lounge, where he was again too apprehensive to come to the boil, and finally up to my room. One could still see the tennis courts; but the tennis courts couldn't see us.

He sat, like Conrad, in the larger of the two armchairs, seeing himself as a dominant character. The slablike features made no provision for subtle nuances of feeling to show in changing muscle tensions round eyes, mouth, or jawline, so that I found it as nearly impossible as always to guess what he was thinking. The over-all impression was of aggression and worry having a dingdong: the result, apparent indecision about whether to attack or placate.

"Look," he said, in the end, "what are you going to tell Mrs. Cavesey when you get back to England?"

I considered. "I haven't decided."

He thrust his face forward like a bulldog. "Don't you go telling her to change her trainer."

"Why precisely not?"

"There's nothing wrong with the way I train them."

"They look well," I agreed. "And they run stinking. Most owners would have sent them to someone else long ago."

"It's not my fault they don't win," he asserted heavily. "You tell her that. That's what I came to say. You tell her it's not my fault."

"You would lose their training fees if they went," I said. "And you would lose face, perhaps. But you would gain freedom from the fear of being prosecuted for fraud."

"See here, Mister," he began angrily, but I interrupted him.

"Alternatively, you could sack your head boy, Barty."

Whatever he had been going to say remained unsaid. His traplike mouth dropped open.

"Should you decide to sack Barty," I said conversationally, "I could advise Mrs. Cavesey to leave the horses where they are."

He shut his mouth. There was a long pause while most of the aggression oozed away and a tired sort of defeatism took its place.

"I can't do that," he said sullenly, not denying the need for it.

"Because of a threat that you will be warned off?" I suggested. "Or because of the profit to come?"

"Look, Mister—"

"See that Barty leaves before I go home," I said pleasantly.

He stood up heavily, and gave me a hard stare which got him nowhere very much. Breathing loudly through his nose, he was inarticulate; and I couldn't guess from his expression whether what hung fire on his tongue was a stream of invective, a defense in mitigation, or even a plea for help.

He checked through the window that his buddy Danilo was still on the courts, then turned away abruptly and departed from my room without another word: a man on a three-pronged toasting fork if ever I saw one.

I returned to the terrace, found Clifford Wenkins walking indecisively about, peering at strangers behind their newspapers.

"Mr. Wenkins," I called.

He looked up, nodded nervously, and scuttled around tables and chairs to reach me.

"Good morning—er—Link," he began, and half held out one hand, too far away for me to shake it. I sketched an equally noncommittal welcome. His best friend must have been telling him, I thought.

We sat at one of the small tables in the shade of a yellow-and-white sun awning, and he agreed that—er—yes, a beer would be fine. He pulled another untidy wad of papers out of an inner pocket. Consulting them seemed to give him strength.

"Er—Worldic have decided ... Er—they think it would be best, I mean, to hold the reception before—er—the film, you see."

I saw. They were afraid I would vanish during the showing if they arranged things the other way round.

"Here—er—is a list of people—er—invited by Worldic. And here—somewhere here—ah, yes, here is the press list and—er—a list of people who have bought tickets to the reception. ... We limited the—er—numbers, but we have—er—had—I mean—it may be—perhaps—just a bit of a *crush,* if you see what I mean."

He sweated. Mopped up with a neatly folded white square. Waited, apparently, for me to burn. But what could I say? I'd arranged it myself; and I suppose I was grateful that people actually wanted to come.

"Er—if that's all right . . . I mean—well—there are still some tickets left—er—for the première itself, you see—er—some at twenty rand."

"Twenty rand?" I said. "Surely that's too much?"

"It's for charity," he said quickly. "Charity."

"What charity?"

"Oh—er—let's see. I've got it here somewhere." But he couldn't find it. "Anyway—for charity—so Worldic want you to . . . I mean, because there are still some tickets, you see, to—er—well, some sort of publicity stunt."

"No," I said.

He looked unhappy. "I told them—but they said—er—well . . ." He faded away like a pop song, and didn't say that Worldic's attitude to actors made the K.G.B. seem paternal.

"Where is the reception to be?" I asked.

"Oh—er—opposite the Wideworld Cinema, in the Klipspringer Heights Hotel. I—er—I think you will like it. . . . I mean—it is one of the best—er—hotels in Johannesburg."

"Fine," I said. "I'll be back here by, say, six o'clock next Tuesday evening. You could ring me here for final arrangements."

"Oh, yes—er," he said, "but—er—Worldic said they would like—er—to know where you are staying—er—in the Kruger Park."

"I don't know," I said.

"Well, er—could you find out?" He looked unhappy. "Worldic said—er—on no account—should I not find out. . . ."

"Oh. Very well," I said. "I'll let you know."

"Thank you," he gasped. "Now—er—well—I mean—

er—" He was working himself into a worse lather than ever over what he was trying to say next. My mind had framed one large "NO" before the thought of Worldic on his tail had goaded him to get it out.

"We—well, that is to say—Worldic have fixed a—er—photographic—session for you. . . . I mean—well, this afternoon, in fact."

"What photographic session?" I asked ominously.

He had another mop. "Just—well—photographs."

He had a terrible time explaining, and a worse time when I got it straight, that what Worldic wanted were some pictures of me reclining in bathing trunks under a sun umbrella beside a bosomy model in a bikini.

"You just run along and tell Worldic that their promotion ideas are fifty years out-of-date if they think cheesecake will sell twenty-rand seats."

He sweated.

"And furthermore you can tell Worldic that one more damn-fool suggestion and I'll never again turn up at anything they handle."

"B-But," he stuttered. "You see—after those pics in the newspapers—of you giving Katya the kiss of life—after that, see, we were flooded—simply flooded—with inquiries. . . . And all the cheaper seats went in a flash—and the reception tickets, too—all went. . . ."

"But that," I said slowly and positively, "was not a publicity stunt."

"Oh, no." He gulped. "Oh, no. Of course not. Oh, no. Oh, no." He rocked to his feet, knocking his chair over. The beads were running down his forehead and his eyes looked wild. He was on the point, the very point, of panic flight when Danilo and Sally came breezily back from the courts.

"Hullo, Mr. Wenkins," Sally said in her adolescent unperceptive way. "I say, you look almost as hot and sweaty as we do."

Wenkins gave her a glazed, mesmerized look and fumbled around with his handkerchief. Danilo looked at him piercingly and thoughtfully and made no remark at all.

"Well—I'll—er, tell them—but they won't—like it."

"You tell them," I agreed. "No stunts."

"No stunts," he echoed weakly; but I doubted whether he would ever have the nerve to pass on the message.

Sally watched his back view weave unsteadily into the Club as she sprawled exhaustedly in her garden chair.

"I say, he does get himself into a fuss, don't you think? Were you bullying the poor lamb, Link?"

"He's a sheep, not a lamb."

"A silly sheep," Danilo said vaguely, as if his thoughts were somewhere else.

"Could I have some orange juice?" Sally said.

Evan and Conrad arrived before the waiter, and the drinks order expanded. Evan was at his most insistent, waving his arms about and laying down the law to Conrad in the usual dominating I-am-the-director-and-the-rest-of-you-are-scum manner. Conrad looked half patient, half irritated; lighting cameramen were outranked by directors, but they didn't have to like it.

"Symbolism," Evan was saying fiercely. "Symbolism is what the film is all about. And post office towers are the new phallic symbol of national strength. Every virile country has to have its revolving restaurant."

"It might be just because every country has one that the one in Johannesburg is not news," Conrad murmured, in a tone a little too carefully unargumentative.

"The tower is *in*," stated Evan with finality.

"Even if you can't find an elephant that shape," I said, nodding.

Conrad choked and Evan glared.

Sally said, "What is a phallic symbol?" And Danilo told her kindly to look it up in the dictionary.

I asked Evan where exactly we would be staying in the Kruger Park, so that I could be found if necessary.

"Don't expect me to help," he said unhelpfully. "The production department made the bookings months ago.

Several different camps, starting in the south and working north, I believe."

Conrad added casually, "We do have a list, back at the hotel. I could copy it out for you, dear boy."

"It isn't important," I said. "It was only Worldic who wanted it."

"Not important!" Evan exclaimed. "If Worldic want it, of course they must have it." Evan had no reservations toward companies that might screen his masterpieces. "Conrad can copy the list and send it to them direct."

I looked at Conrad in amusement. "To Clifford Wenkins, then," I suggested. "It was he who asked."

Conrad nodded shortly. Copying the list from friendliness was one thing and on Evan's orders another; I knew exactly how he felt.

"I don't suppose you are intending to bring the chauffeur Worldic gave you," Evan said bossily to me. "There won't be any rooms for him."

I shook my head. "No," I said mildly. "I'm hiring a car to drive myself."

"All right, then."

Even on a fine Tuesday morning, with a healthy gin half drunk and no pressure on him at all, he still flourished the hot eyes like lances and curled his fingers so that the tendons showed tight. The unruly curly hair sprang out vigorously like Medusa's snakes, and the very air around him seemed to quiver from his energy output.

Sally thought him fascinating. "You'll love it in the game park," she told him earnestly. "The animals are so sweet."

Evan only knew how to deal with girls that young if he could bully them in front of a camera; and the idea that animals could be sweet instead of symbolic seemed to nonplus him.

"Er . . ." he said uncertainly, and sounded exactly like Wenkins.

Conrad cheered up perceptibly, smoothed his mustache, and looked on Sally benignly. She gave him an uncomplicated smile and turned to Danilo.

"You'd love it, too," she said. "Next time you come to South Africa, we must take you down there."

Danilo could scarcely wait. Conrad asked him how much longer he was staying this time, and Danilo said a week or so, he guessed, and Sally insisted anxiously that he was staying until after Link's première; surely he remembered he was going to the reception with the van Hurens. Danilo remembered; he sure was.

He grinned at her. She blossomed. I hoped that the sun kid dealt in compassion alongside the mathematics.

Evan and Conrad stayed for lunch, endlessly discussing the locations they had picked throughout the city. They were, it appeared, going to incorporate a lot of *cinéma vérité,* with Conrad humping around a hand-held Arriflex to film life as it was lived. By the end of the cheese, the whole film—symbolism, elephants, and all—seemed to me doomed to be a crashing bore.

Conrad's interest was principally technical. Mine was nonexistent. Evan's, as usual, inexhaustible.

"So we'll take the Arriflex with us, of course," he was telling Conrad. "We may see unrepeatable shots. It would be stupid not to be equipped."

Conrad agreed. They also discussed sound-recording equipment and decided to take that, too. The production department had fixed up for a park ranger to show them round in a Land-Rover, so there would be room to use everything comfortably.

Anything which they could not cram into their hired station wagon for the journey down, they said, could go in my car, couldn't it? It could. I agreed to drive to their hotel first thing in the morning to embark the surplus.

When they had gone, I paid off the car and chauffeur Worldic had arranged, and hired a modest self-drive sedan instead. A man from the hiring company brought it to the Iguana, showed me the gear system, said it was a new car only just run in and that I should have no trouble with it, and departed with the chauffeur.

I went for a practice drive, got lost, bought a map, and found my way back. The car was short on power uphill, but very stable on corners: a car for Sunday afternoons, airing Grandma in a hat.

12

The map and the car took me to Roderick's flat just as it was getting dark.

I tested the brakes before I set off, the car having stood alone in the car park for hours. Nothing wrong with them, of course. I sneered inwardly at myself for being so silly.

Roderick's flat was on the sixth floor.

It had a balcony.

Roderick invited me out first thing to look at the view.

"It looks marvelous at this time of night," he said, "with the lights springing up in every direction. In the daytime, there are too many factories and roads and mining tips, unless of course you find the sinews of trade stimulating. . . . And soon it will be too dark to see the shape of things in the dusk."

I hovered, despite myself, on the threshold.

"Come on," he said. "Are you afraid of heights?"

"No."

I stepped out then, and the view lived up to his commercial. The balcony faced south, with the kite-shaped Southern Cross flying on its side in the sky straight ahead;

and orange lights stretching like a chain away toward Durban down the motorway.

Roderick was not leaning on the pierced ironwork which edged the balcony. With part of my mind shivering and the rest telling me not to be such an ass, I kept my weight nearer the building than his; I felt guilty of mistrust and yet couldn't trust, and saw that suspicion was a wrecker.

We went in. Of course we went in. Safely. I could feel muscles relax in my jaw and abdomen that I hadn't known were tense. Silly fool, I thought, and tried to shut out the fact that for both the mike and mine misfortunes, Roderick had been there.

His flat was small but predictably full of impact. A black sack chair flopped on a pale olive carpet; khaki-colored walls sprouted huge brass lamp brackets between large canvases of ultra-simple abstracts in brash challenging colors; a low glass-topped table stood before an imitation tiger-skin sofa of stark square construction: and an Andy Warholish imitation can of beer stood waist high in one corner. Desperately trendy, the whole thing; giving, like its incumbent, the impression that way out was where it was all at, man, and if you weren't out there as far as you could go you might as well be dead. It seemed a foregone conclusion that he smoked pot.

Naturally, he had expensive stereo. The music he chose was less underground than could be got in London, but the mix of anarchy and self-pity still came across strongly in the nasal voices. I wondered whether it was just part of the image, or whether he sincerely enjoyed it.

"Drink?" he offered, and I said yes, please.

Campari and soda, bittersweet pink stuff. He took it for granted I would like it.

"Katya won't be long. She had some recording session or other."

"Is she all right now?"

"Sure," he said. "A hundred percent." He underplayed the relief, but I remembered his tormented tears; real emotions still lived down there under the with-it front.

He was wearing another pair of pasted-on trousers, and a blue ruffled close-fitting shirt with lacing instead of buttons. As casual clothes, they were as deliberate as signposts: the rugged male in his sexual finery. I supposed my own clothes, too, made a statement, as indeed everyone's did, always.

Katya's statement was as clear as a trumpet, and said "Look at me."

She arrived like a gust of bright and breezy show biz, wearing an eye-stunning yellow catsuit, which flared widely from the knees in black-edged ruffles. She looked like a flamenco dancer split up the middle, and she topped up the impression with a high tortoise-shell mantilla comb pegged like a tiara into her mop of hair.

Stretching out her arms, she advanced on me with life positively spurting from every pore, as if instead of harming her the input of electric current had doubled her vitality.

"Link, darling, how marvelous," she said extravagantly. And she had brought someone with her.

The barriers in my mind rose immediately like a hedge and prickled away all evening. Roderick and Katya had planted a bombshell to lead me astray, and were betraying their intention through the heightened mischief in Katya's manner. I didn't like the game, but I was an old hand at it, and nowadays I never lost. I sighed regretfully for the quiet no-fuss dinner which Roderick had promised. Too much ever to hope for, I supposed.

The girl was ravishing, with cloudy dark hair and enormous slightly myopic-looking eyes. She wore a soft floaty garment, floor length and green, which swirled and lay against her as she moved, outlining now a hip, now a breast, and all parts in quite clearly good shape.

Roderick was watching my reactions obliquely, while pretending to pour out more Camparis.

"This is Melanie," Katya said, as if inventing Venus from the waves; and there was perhaps a touch of the Botticellis in the graceful neck.

Christened Mabel, no doubt, I said to myself uncharitably, and greeted her with a lukewarm smile and a conventional handshake. Melanie was not a girl to be put off by a cool reception. She gave me a gentle flutter of lengthy lashes, a sweet curve of soft pink lips, and a smoldering promise in the smoky eyes. I thought, She's done this sort of thing before, and she is as aware of her power as I am when I act.

Melanie just happened to sit beside me on the tiger-skin sofa, stretching out languorously so that the green material revealed the whole slender shape. Just happened to have no lighter of her own, so that I had to help her with Roderick's orange globe table model. Just happened to have to cup my hand in both of hers to guide the flame to the end of her cigarette. Just happened to steady herself with a hand on my arm as she leaned forward to flick off ash.

Katya gaily sparkled and Roderick filled my glass with gin when he thought I wasn't looking, and I began to wonder where he had hidden the tape recorder. If this little lot was to be off the record, I was a plumber's mate.

Dinner was laid with candles on a square black table in a mustard-painted dining alcove. The food was great and the talk provocative, but mostly the three of them tossed the ball among themselves while I replied when essential with murmurs and smiles, which couldn't be picked on as quotes.

Melanie's scent was as subtle as Joy, and Roderick had laced my wine with brandy. He watched and spoke and attended to me with friendly eyes, and waited for me to deliver myself up. Go stuff the Rand *Daily Star,* I thought; my friend Roderick is a bastard and my tongue is my own.

Something of my awareness must have shown in my eyes, for a thoughtful look suddenly crossed Roderick's forehead and he changed his tack in two sentences from sexual innuendo to meaningful social comment.

He said, "What do you think of apartheid, now that you've been here a week?"

"What do you?" I replied. "Tell me about it. You three who live here. You tell *me.*"

Roderick shook his head, and Katya said it was what visitors thought that mattered, and only Melanie, who was playing different rules, came across with the goods.

"Apartheid," she said earnestly, "is necessary."

Roderick made a negative movement, and I asked, "In what way?"

"It means living separately," she said. "It doesn't mean that one race is better than the other, just that they're different, and should remain so. All the world seems to think that white South Africans hate the blacks and try to repress them, but it is not true. We care for them . . . and the phrase 'Black is beautiful' was thought up by white Africans to give black Africans a sense of being important as individuals."

I was intensely surprised, but Roderick reluctantly nodded. "That's true. The Black Power movement have adopted it as their own, but they didn't invent it. You might say, I suppose, that the phrase has achieved everything it was intended to, and a bit more besides."

"To read foreign papers," Melanie said indignantly, warming to her subject, "you would think the blacks are a lot of illiterate cheap labor. And it isn't true. Schooling is compulsory for both races, and factories pay the rate for the job, regardless of skin color. And that," she added, "was negotiated by the white trade unionists."

I liked her a lot better since she'd forgotten the sexpot role. The dark eyes held fire as well as smoke, and it was a change to hear someone passionately defending her country.

"Tell me more," I said flippantly.

"Oh . . ." She looked confused for a moment, then took a fresh hold on enthusiasm, like a horse getting its second wind. "Black people have everything the same as white people. Everything that they want to have. Only a minority have big houses, because the majority don't like them: they like to live out-of-doors, and only go into shelters to sleep. But they have cars and businesses and holidays and hospitals and hotels and cinemas—everything like that."

The white people on the whole had more money, I

thought; and undoubtedly more freedom of action. I opened my mouth to make some innocuous remark about the many entrance doors marked "Non-Whites" and "Whites Only," but Melanie jumped right in to forestall any adverse comment, which was not in the least what Roderick wanted. He frowned at her. She was too busy to notice.

"I know what you're going to say," she said inaccurately. "You're going to talk about injustice. Everyone from England always does. Well, certainly, of course there are injustices. There are in every country in the world, including yours. Injustices make the headlines. Justice is not news. People come here purposely seeking for injustice, and of course they find it. But they never report on the good things; they just shut their eyes and pretend there aren't any."

I looked at her thoughtfully. There was truth in what she said.

"Every time a country like England attacks our way of life," she said, "they do more harm than good. You can feel the people here close their ranks and harden their attitude. It is stupid. It slows down the progress our country is gradually making toward partnership between the races. The old rigid type of apartheid is dying out, you know, and in five or ten years' time it will only be the militants and extremists on both sides who take it seriously. They shout and thump, and the foreign press listens and pays attention, like they always do to crackpots, and they don't see—or, at any rate, they never mention—the slow quiet change for the better which is going on here."

I wondered how she would feel about it if she were black: even if things were changing, there still was not over-all equality of opportunity. Blacks could be teachers, doctors, lawyers, priests. They couldn't be jockeys. Unfair, unfair.

Roderick, waiting in vain for me to jump in with both "What are your views, Link?" feet, was driven again to a direct question.

I smiled at him.

"I belong to a profession," I said, "which never discriminates against blacks or Jews or women or Catholics or Protestants or bug-eyed monsters, but only against non-members of Equity."

Melanie looked blank about Equity but she had a word to say about Jews.

"Whatever white South Africans may be accused of," she contended, "we have never sent six million blacks to the gas chamber."

Which was rather like saying, I thought frivolously, that one might have measles, but had never infected anyone with whooping cough.

Roderick gave up angling for a quotable political commitment and tried to bounce Melanie back into sultry seduction. Her own instincts were telling her she would get farther with me if she laid off the sex, because the doubt showed clearly in her manner as she attempted to do as he wanted. But evidently it was important to them both that she should persevere, and she refused to be discouraged by my lack of answering spark. She smiled a meek feminine smile to deprecate every opinion she had uttered, and bashfully lowered the thick black lashes.

Katya and Roderick exchanged eye signals as blinding as lighthouses on a dark night, and Katya said she was going to make coffee. Roderick said he would help, and why didn't Melanie and Link move over to the sofa; it was more comfortable than sitting round the table.

Melanie smiled shyly. I admired the achievement; she was as shy underneath as a sergeant major. She draped herself beautifully over the sofa, with the green material swirling closely across the perfect bosom which rose and fell gently with every breath. She noted the direction of my eyes and smiled with pussycat satisfaction.

Premature, dearest Melanie, premature, I thought.

Roderick carried in a tray of coffee cups and Katya went out onto the balcony. When she came in, she shook her head. Roderick poured out the coffee and Katya handed it round; the suppressed inner excitement, absent during dinner, was fizzing away again in the corners of her smile.

I looked at my watch. Quarter past ten.

I said, "I must be going soon. Early start tomorrow morning, I'm afraid."

Katya said quickly, "Oh, no, you can't go yet, Link," and Roderick handed me a bulbous glass with enough brandy to sink a battleship. I took a sip but made it look like a swallow, and reflected that if I'd drunk everything he'd given me I would have been in no state to drive away.

Melanie kicked off her golden slippers and flexed her toes. On them she wore pearly pink nail varnish and nothing else, and with a quick flash of bare ankle and calf she managed to plant the idea in my mind that under the green shift there were no other clothes.

The coffee was as good as the dinner; Katya was more expert a cook than a conspirator. Within twenty minutes, she again strolled out onto the balcony, and this time, when she came back, the message was a nod.

I looked at all three of them, wondering. Roderick with his old-young face, Katya yellow-frilly and irresponsible, Melanie conscientiously weaving her web. They had laid some sort of trap. The only thing was . . . what?

Twenty to eleven. I finished my coffee, stood up, and said, "I really must go now."

This time, there was no resistance. They all three uncurled themselves to their feet.

"Thank you," I said, "for a great evening."

They smiled.

"Marvelous food," I said to Katya.

She smiled.

"Splendid drinks," I said to Roderick.

He smiled.

"Superb company," I said to Melanie.

She smiled.

Not a really genuine smile among them. They had watchful, expectant eyes. My mouth, for all the available liquid, felt dry.

We moved toward the lobby, which was an extension of the sitting room.

Melanie said, "Time I was going, too. Roderick, would you order me a taxi?"

"Sure, love," he said easily, and then, as if the thought was just striking, "but you go the same way as Link. I'm sure he would give you a lift."

They all looked at me, smiling.

"Of course," I said. What else. What else could I say?

The smiles went on and on.

Melanie scooped up a tiny wrap from beside the front door, and Roderick and Katya saw us down the hall and into the lift, and were still waving farewell as the doors closed between us. The lift sank. One of those automatic lifts which stopped at every floor one had preselected. I pressed G for ground, and at G for ground it stopped.

Politely I let Melanie out first. Then I said, "I say—terribly sorry I've left my signet ring on the washbasin in Roderick's bathroom. I'll just dash back for it. You wait there, I won't be a second."

The doors were closing before she could demur. I pressed the buttons for floors 2 and 6. Got out at 2. Watched the pointer begin to slide toward Roderick's floor at 6, and skipped quickly through the doors of the service stairs at the back of the hall.

The unadorned concrete and ironwork steps wound down round a small steep well and let me out into an area full of stacked laundry baskets, central heating boilers, and rows of garbage cans. Out in the narrow street behind the covered yard, I turned left, skirted the whole of the next-door block at a fast pace, and finally, more slowly, inconspicuously walked in the shadows back toward Roderick's.

I stopped in a doorway a hundred yards away, and watched.

There were four men in the street, waiting. Two opposite the front entrance of Roderick's apartment block. Two others patiently standing near my hired car. All of them carried objects which gleamed in the street lamps, and whose shapes I knew all too well.

Melanie came out of the apartment block and hurried

across the road to talk to two of the men. The green dress clung to her body and appeared diaphanous to the point of transparency in the quality of light in the street. She and the men conferred agitatedly, and there was a great deal of shaking of heads.

All three of them suddenly looked up, and I followed the direction of their gaze. Roderick and Katya were standing out on the balcony, calling down. I was too far away to hear the exact words, but the gist was entirely guessable. The quarry had got away, and none of them was pleased.

Melanie and the two men turned and walked in my direction, but only as far as the other two beside my car. They all five went into a huddle which could produce no happiness, and in the end Melanie walked back alone and disappeared into the flats.

I sighed wryly. Roderick was no murderer. He was a newspaperman. The four men had come armed with cameras. Not knives. Not guns.

Not my life they were after; just my picture.

Just my picture outside a block of flats at night alone with a beautiful girl in a totally revealing dress.

I looked thoughtfully at the four men beside my car, decided the odds were against it, turned on my heel, and quietly walked away.

Back at the Iguana Rock (by taxi), I telephoned Roderick.

He sounded subdued.

I said, "Damn your bloody eyes."

"Yes."

"Have you got this telephone bugged?"

A pause. Then, on a sigh again, he said, "Yes."

"Too late for honesty, my friend."

"Link—"

"Forget it," I said. "Just tell me why."

"My paper—"

"No," I said. "Newspapers don't get up to such tricks. That was a spot of private enterprise."

A longer pause.

"I guess I owe it to you," he said slowly. "We did it for Clifford Wenkins. The little runt is scared silly by Worldic, and he begged us, in return for favors he has done us from time to time, to set you up for him. He said Worldic would sack him if he couldn't persuade you to do a girly session to sell their twenty-rand seats, and he had asked you, and you had absolutely refused. Melanie is our top model girl, and he got her to help in a good cause."

"That Wenkins," I said bitterly, "would sell his soul for publicity stunts."

"I'm sorry, Link."

"Not as sorry as he will be," I said ominously.

"I promised him I wouldn't tell you."

"Stuff both of you," I said violently, and rattled the receiver into its cradle.

13

The next morning, the Iguana management having kindly sent someone with the keys to fetch my hired car from outside Roderick's flat, I packed what little I would need for the Kruger Park, and chuntered round to Evan and Conrad's hotel.

The loading of their station wagon was in process of being directed by Evan as if it were the key scene in a prestige production, and performed by Conrad at his most eccentric. Boxes, bags, and black zipped equipment littered the ground for a radius of ten yards.

"Dear boy," Conrad said as I approached, "for God's sake get some ice."

"Ice?" I echoed vaguely.

"Ice." He pointed to a yellow plastic box about two feet by one. "In there. For the film."

"What about beer?"

He gave me a sorrowful, withering glance. "Beer in the red one, dear boy."

The red thermal box had had priority; had already been zipped tight shut and lifted onto the car. Smiling, I went into the hotel on the errand and returned with a large plastic bagful. Conrad laid the ice pack in the yellow box and carefully stacked his raw stock on top. The yellow box joined the red one, and Evan said that at this rate we wouldn't reach the Kruger by nightfall.

At eleven, the station wagon was full to the gunnels but the ground was still littered with that extraordinary collection of wires, boxes, tripods, and clips which seem to accompany cameramen everywhere.

Evan waved his arms, as if by magic the whole lot would leap into order. Conrad pulled his mustache dubiously. I opened the boot of my saloon, shoveled everything in unceremoniously, and told him he could sort it all out when we arrived.

After that we adjourned for thirst quenchers, and finally got the wheels on the road at noon. We drove east by north for about five hours and descended from the high Johannesburg plateau down to a few hundred feet above sea level. The air grew noticeably warmer on every long downhill stretch, which gave rise to three or four more stops for sustenance. Conrad's cubic capacity rivaled the Bantus'.

By five, we arrived at the Numbi gate, the nearest way into the park. The Kruger itself stretched a further two hundred miles north and fifty east, with nothing to keep the animals in except their own wish to stay. The Numbi gate consisted of a simple swinging barrier guarded by two khaki-uniformed black Africans and a small office. Evan produced passes for two cars and reservations for staying in the camps, and with grins and salutes the passes were stamped and the gates swung open.

Brilliant scarlet and magenta bougainvillaea just inside proved misleading: the park itself was tinder dry and thorny brown after months of sun and no rain. The narrow road stretched ahead into a baked wilderness where the only man-made thing in sight was the tarmac itself.

"Zebras!" shouted Evan, winding down his window and screaming out of it.

I followed his pointing finger, and saw the dusty herd of them standing patiently under bare-branched trees, slowly swinging their tails and merging uncannily into the striped shade.

Conrad had a map, which was just as well. We were headed for the nearest camp, Pretoriuskop, but roads wound and criss-crossed as we approached it, unfinished dry earth roads leading off at tangents to vast areas inhabited believably by lion, rhinoceros, buffalo, and crocodile.

And, of course, elephant.

The camp turned out to be an area of several dozen acres, enclosed by a stout wire fence, and containing nothing so camp-like as tents. Rather like Butlin's gone native, I thought: clusters of round, brick-walled, thatched-roofed cabins like pink-colored drums with wide-brimmed hats on.

"Rondavels," Evan said in his best dogmatic manner, waving a hand at them. He checked in at the big reception office and drove off to search for the huts with the right numbers. There were three of them: one each. Inside, two beds, a table, two chairs, fitted cupboard, shower room, and air conditioning. Every mod con in the middle of the jungle.

Evan banged on my door and said come on out, we were going for a drive. The camp locked its gates for the night at six-thirty, he said, which gave us forty minutes to go and look at baboons.

"It will take too long to unpack the station wagon," he said. "So we will all go in your car."

I drove and they gazed steadfastly out of the windows. There were some distant baboons scratching themselves in the evening sunlight on a rocky hill, and a herd of impala munching away at almost leafless bushes, but not an elephant in sight.

"We'd better go back before we get lost," I said, but even then we whizzed through the gates only seconds before closing time.

"What happens if you're late?" I asked.

"You have to spend the night outside," Evan said positively. "Once the gate is closed, it's closed."

Evan, as usual, seemed to be drawing information out

of the air, though he gave the game away later by producing an information booklet he had been given in reception. The booklet also said not to wind down windows and scream "Zebra!" out of them, as the animals didn't like it. Wild animals, it appeared, thought cars were harmless and left them alone, but were liable to bite any bits of humans sticking out.

Conrad had had to unpack the whole station wagon to unload the red beer box, which was likely to reverse his priorities. We sat round a table outside the huts, cooling our throats in the warm air and watching the dark creep closer between the rondavels. Even with Evan there, it was peaceful enough to unjangle the screwiest nerves ... and lull the wariest mind into a sense of security.

Thursday, the following day, we set off at daybreak and breakfasted at the next camp, Skukusa, where we were to stay that night.

Skukusa was larger and boasted executive status rondavels, which Evan's production company had naturally latched on to. They had also engaged the full-time attendance of a park ranger named Haagner for the day, which would have been splendid had he not been an Afrikaner with incomplete English. He was big, slow-moving, quiet, and unemotional, the antithesis of Evan's fiery zeal for allegory.

Evan shot questions and had to wait through silences for his answers; no doubt Haagner was merely translating the one into Afrikaans in his head, formulating the other, and translating that into English, but the delay irritated Evan from the start. Haagner treated Evan with detachment and refused to be hurried, which gave Conrad the (decently concealed) satisfaction of an underdog seeing his master slip on a banana skin.

We set off in Haagner's Range Rover, accompanied by the Arriflex, a tape recorder, half a dozen smaller cameras, and the red thermal box loaded with a mixed cargo of film, beer, fruit, and sandwiches in plastic bags. Evan had brought sketch pads, maps, and notebooks, and six times remarked that the company should have equipped him with a secretary. Conrad murmured that we should be glad that we weren't equipped with Drix Goddart, but from the sour look Evan slid me he didn't necessarily agree.

"Olifant," Haagner said, pointing, having been three times told of the aim of the expedition.

He stopped the van. "There, in the valley."

We looked. A lot of trees, a patch of green, a winding river.

"There, man," he said.

Eventually our untrained eyes saw them; three dark hunched shapes made small by distance, flapping a lazy ear behind a bush.

"Not near enough," Evan said disgustedly. "We must get nearer."

"Not here," said Haagner. "They are across the river. The Sabie River. *'Sabie'* is Bantu word; it means 'fear.' "

I looked at him suspiciously, but he was not provoking Evan in any way; simply imparting information. The slow peaceful-looking water wound through the valley and looked as unfearful as the Thames.

Evan had no eyes for the various antelope-like species Haagner pointed out, or for the blue jays or turkey buzzards or vervet monkeys or wildebeests, and particularly not for the herds of gentle impala. Only the implicitly violent took his attention: the vulture, the hyena, the wart hog, the possibility of lion, and the scarcity of cheetah.

And, of course, *olifants.* Evan adopted the Afrikaans word as his own and rolled it round his tongue as if he alone had invented it. *Olifant* droppings on the road (fresh, said Haagner) excited him almost to orgasm. He insisted on stopping there and reversing for a better view, and on Conrad sticking the Arriflex lens out of the window and exposing about fifty feet of film from different angles and with several focal lengths.

Haagner, patiently repositioning the van for every shot, watched these antics and clearly thought Evan unhinged, and I laughed internally until my throat ached. Had the obliging elephant returned, Evan would no doubt have directed him to defecate again for Scene 1, Take 2. He would have seen nothing odd in it.

Evan left the heap reluctantly and was working out how to symbolize it in an utterly meaningful way. Conrad said he could do with a beer, but Haagner pointed ahead and said "Onder-Sabie," which turned out to be another camp like the others.

"Olifant in Saliji River," said Haagner, coming back from a chat with some colleagues. "If we go now, you see them perhaps."

Evan swept us away from the shady table and our half-empty glasses and scurried forth again into the increasing noonday heat. All around us, more sensible mortals were fanning themselves and contemplating siesta, but *olifants,* with Evan, came before sense.

The Range Rover was as hot as an oven.

"It is hot today," Haagner said. "Hotter tomorrow. Summer is coming. Soon we will have the rain, and all the park will be green."

Evan, alarmed, said, "No, no. The park must be burned up, just like this. Inhospitable land, bare, hungry, predatory, aggressive, and cruel. Certainly not soft and lush."

Haagner understood less than a tenth. After a long pause, he merely repeated the bad news: "In one month, after the rains start, the park will be all green. Then much water. Now not much. All small rivers are dry. We find *olifant* near big rivers. In Mnondozi."

He drove several miles and stopped beside a large wooden sun shelter built high at the end of a valley. Below, the Mnondozi River stretched away straight ahead, and the *olifants* had done Evan proud. A large family of them were playing in the water, squirting each other through their trunks and taking care of their kids.

As it was an official picnic place especially built in an area of cleared ground, we were all allowed out of the car. I stretched myself thankfully and dug into the red box for a spot of irrigation. Conrad had a camera in one hand and a beer in the other, and Evan brandished his enthusiasm over us all like a whip.

Haagner and I sat in ninety degrees in the shade at one of the small scattered tables and ate some of the packed sandwiches. He had warned Evan not to go too far from the shelter while filming, as it presented an open invitation to a hungry lion, but Evan naturally believed that he would not meet one; and he didn't. He took Conrad, plus Arriflex, fifty yards downhill into the bush for some closer shots, and Haagner called him urgently to come back, telling me his job would be lost if Evan were.

Conrad soon climbed up again, mopping drops from his brow which were not all heat, and reported that something was grunting down there behind some rocks.

"There are twelve hundred lion in the park," Haagner said. "When hungry, they kill. Lions alone kill thirty thousand animals in the park every year."

"God," said Conrad, visibly losing interest in Evan's whole project.

Eventually Evan returned unscathed, but Haagner regarded him with disfavor.

"More *olifant* in the north," he said. "For *olifant*, you go north." Out of his district, his tone said.

Evan nodded briskly and set his mind at rest.

"Tomorrow. We set off northwards tomorrow, and tomorrow night we stay in a camp called Satara."

Reassured, Haagner drove us slowly back toward Skukusa, conscientiously pointing out animals all the way.

"Could you cross the park on a horse?" I asked Haagner.

He shook his head decisively. "Very dangerous. More dangerous than walking, and walking is not safe." He looked directly at Evan. "If your car break down, wait for next car, and ask people to tell rangers at the next camp. Do not leave your car. Do not walk in the park. Especially do not walk in the park at night. Stay in car all night."

Evan listened to the lecture with every symptom of ignoring it. He pointed instead to one of the several unmetaled side roads we had passed with "No Entry" signs on them, and asked where they led.

"Some go to the many Bantu ranger stations," said Haagner after the pause for translation. "Some to water holes. Some are firebreaks. They are roads for rangers. Not roads for visitors. Do not go down those roads." He looked at Evan, clearly seeing that Evan would not necessarily obey. "It is not allowed."

"Why not?"

"The park is eight thousand square miles. Visitors can get lost."

"We have a map," Evan argued.

"The service roads," Haagner said, stolidly, "are not on the maps."

Evan ate a packet of sandwiches mutinously and rolled down the window to throw out the plastic bag.

"Do not do that," Haagner said sharply enough to stop him.

"Why not?"

"The animals eat them, and choke. No litter must be thrown. It kills the animals."

"Oh, very well," said Evan ungraciously, and handed me the screwed-up bag to return to the red box. The box was clipped shut and tidy, so I shoved it in my pocket. Evan polished off the job of being a nuisance by throwing out instead the half-eaten crust of his cheese-and-tomato.

"Do not feed the animals," said Haagner automatically.

"Why not?" Evan, belligerent, putting on an R.S.P.C.A. face.

"It is unwise to teach animals that cars contain food."

That silenced him flat. Conrad twitched an eyebrow at me and I arranged my face as near impassiveness as one can get while falling about inside.

Owing to an *olifant* waving its ears at us within cricket-ball distance, we did not get back to Skukusa before the gates shut. Evan, oblivious to the fast-setting sun, saw allegories all over the place and had Conrad wasting film by the mile, taking shots through glass. He had wanted Conrad to set up a tripod in the road to get steadier than hand-held pictures, but even he was slightly damped by the frantic quality in Haagner's voice as he told him not to.

"Olifant is the most dangerous of all the animals," he said earnestly, and Conrad equally earnestly assured him that for nothing on earth would he, Conrad, leave the safety of the Range Rover. Haagner wouldn't even have the window open and wanted to drive away at once. It appeared that when *olifants* waved their ears like that they were expressing annoyance, and since they weighed seven tons and could charge at 25 m.p.h., it didn't do to hang about.

Evan didn't believe that any animal would have the gall to attack such important humans as E. Pentelow, director, and E. Lincoln, actor. He persuaded Conrad to get clicking, and Haagner sat there with the engine running and his foot on the clutch. When the elephant finally took one step in our direction, we were off down the road with a jolt that threw Conrad, camera and all, to the floor.

I helped him up, while Evan complained about it to Haagner. The ranger, nearing the end of his patience, stopped the car with an equal jerk and hauled on the hand brake.

"Very well," he said. "We wait."

The elephant came out onto the road, a hundred yards behind us. The big ears were flapping like flags.

Conrad looked back. "Do drive on, dear boy," he said with anxiety in his voice.

Haagner folded his lips. The elephant decided to follow us. He was also accelerating to a trot.

It took more seconds than I cared before Evan cracked. He was saying "For God's sake, where is the Arriflex?" to Conrad when it seemed at last to dawn on him that there might be some real danger.

"Drive away," he said to Haagner urgently. "Can't you see that that animal is charging?"

And it had tusks, I observed.

Haagner, too, decided that enough was enough. He had

the hand brake off and the gears in mesh in one slick movement, and the elephant got a trunkful of dust.

"What about the next car coming along?" I asked. "They'll meet it head on."

Haagner shook his head. "No cars will come this way any more today. It is too late. They will all be near the camps now. And that *olifant,* he will go straight away into the bush. He will not stay on the road."

Conrad looked at his watch. "How long will it take us to get back to Skukusa?"

"With no more stops," Haagner said with bite, "about half an hour."

"But it is six-fifteen already!" Conrad said.

Haagner made a noncommittal movement of his head and didn't answer. Evan appeared subdued into silence and a look of peaceful satisfaction awoke on the Afrikaner's face. For the whole of the rest of the way, it stayed there, first in the quick dusk, then in the reflected glow of the headlights. Before we reached Skukusa, he swung the Range Rover down one of the no-entry side roads, a detour which brought us after a mile or two suddenly and unexpectedly into a village of modern bungalows with tiny little flower gardens and street lighting.

We stared in amazement. A suburb, no less, set down greenly in the brown dry veldt.

"This is the ranger village," Haagner said. "My house is over there, the third down that road. All the whites who work in the camp, and the white rangers, we live here. The Bantu rangers and workers also have villages in the park."

"But the lions," I said. "Are the villages safe, isolated like this?"

He smiled. "It is not isolated." The Range Rover came to the end of the houses, crossed about fifty unlit yards of road, and sped straight into the back regions of Skukusa camp. "But also, no, it is not entirely safe. One must not walk far from houses at night. Lion do not usually come near the gardens—and we have fences round them—but a young Bantu was taken by a lion one night on that short piece of road between our village and camp. I knew him well. He had been told never to walk. . . . It was truly sad."

"Are people often—taken—by lions?" I asked as he pulled up by our rondavels, and we unloaded ourselves, the cameras, and the red box.

"No. Sometimes. Not often. People who work in the park; never visitors. It is safe in cars." He gave Evan one last meaningful stare. "Do not leave your car. To do so is not safe."

Before dinner in the camp restaurant, I put a call through to England. Two hours' delay, they said, but by nine o'clock I was talking to Charlie.

Everything was fine, she said; the children were little hooligans, and she had been to see Nerissa.

"I spent the whole day with her yesterday. Most of the time we just sat, because she felt awfully tired, but she didn't seem to want me to go. I asked her the things you wanted—not all at once, but spread over."

"What did she say?"

"Well, you were right about some things. She did tell Danilo she had Hodgkin's disease. She said she didn't know herself that it was fatal when she told him, but she doesn't think he took much notice, because all he said was that he thought only young people got it."

If he knew that, I thought, he knew a lot more.

"Apparently he stayed with her for about ten days, and they became firm friends. That was how she described it. So she told him, before he went back to America, that she would be leaving him the horses as a personal gift, and also, as he was all the family she had, all the rest of her money after other bequests had been met."

"Lucky old Danilo."

"Yes. Well, he came to see her again, a few weeks ago, late July or early August. While you were in Spain, anyway. She knew by then that she was dying, but she didn't mention it to Danilo. She did show him her will, though, as he seemed interested in it. She said he was so sweet when he had read it, and hoped not to be inheriting for twenty years."

"Little hypocrite."

"I don't know," said Charlie doubtfully, "because although you were right about so much, there is a distinct fly in the woodpile."

"What's that?"

"It can't be Danilo who is making the horses lose. It simply cannot."

"It must be," I said. "And why not?"

"Because when Nerissa told him she was worried about the way they were running, and wished she could find out what was wrong, it was Danilo himself who came up with the idea of sending *you*."

"It can't have been," I exclaimed.

"It definitely was," Charlie said. "She was positive about it. It was Danilo's own suggestion."

"Blast," I said.

"He wouldn't have suggested she send someone to investigate if he'd been nobbling them himself."

"No, I suppose not."

"You sound depressed," she said.

"I haven't any other answers for Nerissa."

"Don't worry. You weren't going to tell her her nephew was up to no good, anyway."

"That's true," I agreed.

"And it wasn't difficult for Danilo to read her will. She leaves it lying around all the time on that marquetry table in the corner of the sitting room. She showed it to me immediately, as soon as I mentioned it, because it interests her a lot. And I saw what keepsakes she is leaving us, if you're interested."

"What are they?" I asked idly, thinking about Danilo.

"She's leaving you her holding in something called Rojedda, and she's leaving me a diamond pendant and some earrings. She showed them to me. They are absolutely beautiful and I told her they were far too much, but she made me try them on so she would see how I looked. She seemed to be so pleased, so happy. . . . Isn't she incredible? I can hardly bear— Oh—oh, dear. . . ."

"Don't cry, darling," I said.

There were some swallowing noises.

"I—can't—help it. She is already much worse than when we saw her before, and she's very uncomfortable. One of her swollen glands is pressing on things in her chest."

"We'll go and see her as soon as I get back."

"Yes." She sniffed away the tears. "God, I do miss you."

"Me, too," I said. "Only one more week. I'll be home a week today, and we'll take the kids down to Cornwall."

After the call, I went outside and walked slowly past our rondavels and out onto the rough grassy area beyond. The African night was very quiet. No roar of traffic from any distant city, just the faint steady hum of the generator supplying Skukusa with electricity, and the energetic music of cicadas.

Nerissa had given me my answers.

I saw what they meant, and I didn't want to believe it.

A gamble. No more, no less.

With my life as the stake.

I went back to telephone and made one more call. Van Huren's manservant said he would see, and Quentin came on the line. I said I knew it was an odd thing to ask, and I would explain why when next I saw him, but could he possibly tell me what size Nerissa's holding in Rojedda was likely to be?

"The same as my own," he said without hesitation. "She has my brother's holding, passed to her by Portia."

I thanked him numbly.

"See you at the première," he said. "We are looking forward to it very much."

For hours, I couldn't go to sleep. Yet where could I be safer than inside a guarded camp, with Evan and Conrad snoring their heads off in the huts next door?

But when I woke up, I was no longer in bed.

I was in the car I had hired in Johannesburg.

The car was surrounded by early daylight in the Kruger National Park. Trees, scrub, and dry grass. Not a rondavel in sight.

Remnants of an ether smell blurred my senses, but one fact was sharp and self-evident.

One of my arms lay through the steering wheel, and my wrists were locked together in a pair of handcuffs.

14

This had to be some ghastly practical joke. Evan, being malicious.

This had to be Clifford Wenkins thinking up some frightful publicity stunt.

This had to be anything but real.

But I knew, deep down in some deathly cold core, that this time there was no girl called Jill coming to set me free.

This time the dying was there to be done. Staring me in the face. Straining already across my shoulders and down my arms.

Danilo was playing for his gold mine.

I felt dizzy and ill. Whatever anesthetic had been used on me had been given crudely. Probably far too much for the purpose. Not that that was likely to worry anyone but me.

For an age, I could think no further. The dizziness kept coming back in clammy pea-green waves. My physical wretchedness blocked any other thought, took up all my attention. Bouts of semiconsciousness brought me each time to a fresh awakening, to renewed awareness of my plight, to malaise and misery.

The first objective observation which pierced the fog was that I had gone to bed wearing shorts, and now had clothes on. The trousers I had worn the day before, and the shirt. Also, upon investigation, socks and slip-on shoes.

The next discovery, which had been knocking at the door of consciousness for some time but had been shut out as unwelcome, was that the car's seat belts were fastened. Across my chest and over my lap, just as in the Special.

They weren't tightly fastened, but I couldn't reach the clip.

I tried. The first of many tries at many things. The first of many frustrations.

I tried to slide my hands out of the handcuffs; but, as before, they were the regulation British police model, designed precisely not to let people slide their hands out. My bones, as before, were too big.

I tried with all my strength to break the steering wheel, but although this one looked flimsy compared with the one in the Special, I still couldn't do it.

I could move a shade more than in the film. The straps were not so tight and there was more room round my legs. Apart from that, there was little difference.

For the first of many times, I wondered how long it would be before anyone set out to look for me.

Evan and Conrad, when they found me missing, would surely start a search. Haagner, surely, would alert every ranger in the park. Someone would come along very soon. Of course they would. And set me free.

The day began to warm up, the sun in a cloudless sky shining brightly through the window on my right. The car was therefore facing north, and I groaned at the thought, because in the Southern Hemisphere the sun shone at midday from the north, and I should have its heat and light full in the face.

Perhaps someone would come before midday.

Perhaps.

The worst of the sickness passed in an hour or two, though the tides of unease ebbed and flowed for much longer. Gradually, however, I began to think again, and to lose the feeling that even if death were already perched on my elbow I was too bilious to care.

Clear thought number one was that Danilo had locked me in this car so that I should die and he would inherit Nerissa's half share in the van Huren gold mine.

Nerissa was leaving her Rojedda holding to me in her will, and Danilo, having read the will, knew.

Danilo was to inherit the residue. Should I die before Nerissa, the Rojedda bequest would be void, and the holding would become part of his residue. Should I live, he stood to lose not only a share of the mine, but hundreds of thousands of pounds besides.

As the law stood then, and would still stand when Nerissa died, estate duty on everything she possessed would be paid out of the residue. Danilo personally stood to lose every penny of the estate duty paid on the inheritance which Nerissa was leaving to me.

If only, I thought uselessly, she had told me what she was doing; I could have explained why she shouldn't. Perhaps she hadn't realized how immensely valuable the Rojedda holding was; she had only recently received it from her sister. Perhaps she hadn't understood how estate duty worked. Certainly, in view of the enjoyment she had found in her long-lost nephew, she had not intended me to prosper out of all proportion at Danilo's expense.

Any accountant would have told her, but wills were usually drawn up by solicitors, not accountants, and solicitors didn't give financial advice.

Danilo, with his mathematical mind, had read the will and seen the barbs in it, as I would have done. Danilo must have begun plotting my death from that very moment.

He had only had to tell me what she had written. But how could he know that? If he himself in reversed positions would have stuck two fingers up in my face, perhaps he thought that I, that anyone, would do that, too.

Nerissa, I thought. Dear, dear Nerissa. Meaning good to everyone, and happily leaving them presents, and landing me, in consequence, in the most unholy bloody mess.

Danilo the gambler. Danilo the bright lad who knew that Hodgkin's disease was fatal. Danilo the little schemer who started by lowering the value of a string of race horses to pay less estate duty on them, and who, when he found that the real stakes were much higher, had the nerve to move at once into the senior league.

I remembered his fascination down the mine, his questions about quantities at lunch, and his tennis game with Sally. He was after the whole works, not just half. Inherit one half and marry the other. No matter that she was only fifteen; in two more years, it would be a highly suitable alliance.

Danilo . . .

I tugged uselessly, in sudden shaking fury, at the obstinate steering wheel. Such cruelty was impossible. How could he—how could anyone—lock a man in a car and leave him to die of heat and thirst and exhaustion? It only happened in films—in one film—*Man in a Car*.

Don't get out of the car, Haagner had said. It is not safe to get out of the car. And a right bloody laugh that was. If I could get out of this car, I would take my chance with the lions.

All that screaming and shouting I had done in the film. I remembered it coldly. The agony of spirit I had imagined and acted. The disintegration of a soul, a process I had dissected into a series of pictures to be presented one by one, until the progression led inexorably to the empty shell of a man too far gone to recover his mind, even if his body were saved.

The man in the Special had been a fictional character. The man had been shown as reacting to every situation throughout the story with impulsive emotion, which was why his weeping fits *in extremis* had been valid. But I was not like the man; in many respects, I was diametrically opposite. I saw the present problem in mainly practical terms, and intended to go on doing so.

Someone, sometime, would find me. I would just have to try, in any way I could, to be alive—and sane—when they did so.

The sun rose high and the car grew hot; but this was only a secondary discomfort.

My bladder was full to bursting.

I could stretch my hands round the wheel to reach and undo the fly zip fastener, which I did. But I couldn't move far on the seat, and even if I managed to open the door with my elbow, there would be no chance of clearing the car. Although there was no sense in it, I postponed the inevitable moment until continence was nearer a pain than a nuisance. But reluctance had its limits. When in the end I had to let go, a lot went as far as the floor, but a lot of it didn't, and I could feel the wetness soaking into my trousers from crotch to knee.

Sitting in a puddle made me extremely angry. Quite unreasonably, forcing me to mess myself seemed a more callous act than putting me in the car in the first place. In the film, we had glossed over this problem as being secondary to the mental state. We had been wrong. It was part of it.

The net result on me was to make me more resolved than ever not to be defeated. It made me mean and revengeful.

It made me hate Danilo.

The morning wore on. The heat became a trial and I got tired of sitting still. I had, however, I told myself, spent three weeks in Spain in precisely this position. There, in fact, it had been much hotter. I willfully ignored the thought that in Spain we had knocked off for lunch.

Lunchtime was pretty near, by my watch. Well ... maybe someone would come. . . .

And how would they get there? I wondered. Ahead of me there was no road, just small trees, dry grass, and scrubby undergrowth. To each side, just the same. But the car must have been driven there, not dropped by passing eagle. . . . Twisting my neck, and consulting the reflection in the mirror, I saw that the road, such as it was, lay directly at my back. It was an earth road showing no sign of upkeep and all too many signs of desertion, and it petered out completely twenty yards or so from where I sat. My car had been driven straight off the end of it into the bush.

In less than a month it would rain; the trees and the grass would grow thick and green, and the road turn to mud. No one would find the car, if it were still there when the rains came.

If I . . . were still there when the rains came.

I shook myself. That way led straight toward the mental state of the man in the film, and of course I had decided to steer clear of it.

Of course.

Perhaps they would send a helicopter. . . .

It was a gray car, nondescript. But surely any car would show up, from the air. There was a small airdrome near Skukusa; I'd seen it marked on the map. Surely Evan would send a helicopter. . . .

But where to? I was facing north, off the end of an abandoned track. I could be anywhere.

Maybe if I did after all make a noise, someone would hear. . . . All those people driving along miles away in their safe little cars with the engines droning and the windows securely shut.

The car's horn . . . useless. It was one of those cars which had to have the ignition switched on before the horn would sound.

In the ignition . . . no keys.

Lunchtime came and went. I could have done with a nice cold beer.

A heavy swishing in the bush behind me sent my head twisting hopefully in its direction. Someone had come. Well, hadn't I known they would?

No human voices, though, exclaimed over me, bringing freedom. My visitor, in fact, had no voice at all, as he was a giraffe.

The great fawn skyscraper with his paler patches rolled rhythmically past the car and began pulling at the sparse leaves scattering the top of the tree straight ahead. He was so close that his bulk shut out the sun, giving me a welcome oasis of shade. Huge and graceful, he stayed for a while, munching peacefully and pausing now and then to bend his great horned head toward the car, peering at it from eyes fringed by outrageously long lashes. The most seductive lady would be reduced to despair by a giraffe's eyelashes.

I found myself talking to him aloud. "Just buzz off over to Skukusa, will you, and get our friend Haagner to come here in his Range Rover at the bloody double."

The sound of my voice startled me, because in it I heard my own conviction. I might hope that Evan or Conrad or Haagner or the merest passing stranger would soon find me, but I didn't believe it. Unconsciously, because of the film, I was already geared to a long wait.

But what I did believe was that in the end someone would come. The peasant would ride by on his donkey, and see the car, and rescue the man. That was the only tolerable ending. The one I had to cling to, and work for.

For in the end, people would search.

If I didn't turn up at the première, there would be questions and checks, and finally a search.

The première was next Wednesday.

Today, I supposed, was Friday.

People could live only six or seven days without water.

I stared somberly at the giraffe. He batted the fantastic eyelashes, shook his head gently as if in sorrow, and ambled elegantly away.

By Wednesday night, I would have spent six whole days without water. No one would find me as soon as Thursday.

Friday or Saturday, perhaps, if they were clever.

It couldn't be done.
It had to be.

When the giraffe took away with him his patch of shade, I realized how fierce the sun had grown. If I did nothing about it, I thought, I would have me a nasty case of sunburn.

The parts of me most relentlessly in the sun were, oddly enough, my hands. As in most hot-country cars, the top third of the windscreen was tinted green against glare, and if I rolled my head back I could get my face out of the direct rays; but they fell unimpeded onto my lap. I solved the worst of that by unbuttoning my shirt cuffs and tucking my hands in the opposite sleeves, like a muff.

After that I debated the wisdom of taking my shoes and socks off, and of opening a window to let in some fresh and cooler air. I could get my feet, one at a time, up to my hands to get my socks off. I could swivel enough in my seat to wind the left-hand window handle with my toes.

It wasn't the thought of invasion by animals that stopped me doing it at once, but the niggling subject of humidity.

The only water available to me for the whole of the time I sat there would be what was contained at that moment in my own body. With every movement and every breath, I was depleting the stock, releasing water into the air about me in the form of invisible water vapor. If I kept the windows shut, the water vapor would mostly stay inside the car. If I opened them, it would instantly be lost.

The outside air, after all those rainless months, was as dry as Prohibition. It seemed to me that though I couldn't stop my body losing a lot of moisture, I could to some extent reuse it. It would take longer, in damper air, for my skin to crack in dehydration. Rebreathing water vapor would go some small way to postponing the time when the mucous linings of nose and throat would dry raw.

So, what with one thing and another, I didn't open the window.

Like a man with an obsession, I turned back again and again to the hope-despair seesaw of rescue, one minute convinced that Evan and Conrad would have sent out sorties the moment they found me gone, the next that they would simply have cursed my rudeness and set off by themselves toward the north, where Evan would become so engrossed with *olifant* that E. Lincoln would fade from his mind like yesterday's news.

No one else would miss me. Everyone back in Johannesburg—the van Hurens, Roderick, Clifford Wenkins—knew I had gone down to the game reserve for the rest of the week. None of them would expect to hear from me. None of them would expect me back before Tuesday.

The only hope I had lay in Evan and Conrad ... and the peasant passing by with his donkey.

At some point during the long afternoon, I thought of seeing if I still had in my trouser pockets the things I had had there the day before. I hadn't emptied the pockets when I undressed; I had just laid my clothes on the second bed.

Investigation showed that my wallet was still buttoned into my rear pocket, because I could feel its shape if I pushed back against the seat. But money, in these circumstances, was useless.

By twisting, lifting myself an inch off the seat, and tugging, I managed to get my right-hand pocket round to center front, and, carefully exploring, brought forth a total prize of a packet of Iguana Rock book matches, with four matches left, a blue rubber band, and a three-inch stub of pencil with no point.

I put all these carefully back where they came from, and reversed the tugging until I could reach into the left-hand pocket.

Two things only in there. A handkerchief ... and the forgotten screwed-up plastic bag from Evan's sandwiches.

"Don't throw plastic bags out of car windows," Haagner had said. "They can kill the animals."

And save the lives of men.

Precious, precious plastic bag.

Never cross a desert without one.

I knew how to get half a cup of water every twenty-four hours from a sheet of plastic in a hot climate, but it couldn't be done by someone strapped into a sitting position inside a car. It needed a hole dug in the ground, a small weight, and something to catch the water in.

All the same, the principle was there, if I could make it work.

Condensation.

The hole-in-the-ground method worked during the night. In the heat of the day, one dug a hole, making it about eighteen inches deep, and in diameter slightly smaller than the available piece of plastic. One placed a cup in the hole, in the center. One spread the sheet of plastic over the hole, and sealed it down round the edges with the dug-out earth or sand. And finally one placed a small stone or some coins on the center of the plastic, weighing it down at a spot directly over the cup.

After that, one waited.

Cooled by the night, the water vapor in the hot air trapped in the hole condensed into visible water droplets, which formed on the cold unporous plastic, trickled downhill to the weighted point, and dripped from there into the cup.

A plastic bagful of hot air should produce a teaspoonful of water by dawn.

It wasn't much.

After a while, I pulled one hand toward me as far as it would go, and leaned forward hard against the seat belt, and found I could reach far enough to blow into the bag if I held its gathered neck loosely with an O of forefinger and thumb.

For probably half an hour, I breathed in through my nose, and out through my mouth, into the plastic bag. At the end of that time, there were hundreds of small water droplets sticking to the inside of the bag—the water vapor out of my lungs, trapped there instead of escaping into the air.

I turned the bag inside out and licked it. It was wet. When I'd sucked off as much as I could, I laid the cool damp surface against my face and, perhaps because of the paltriness of what I had achieved, felt the first deep stab of desolation.

I fished out the blue rubber band again, and while the sunlit air was still hot, filled the bag with air, twisting the neck tight and fastening it with the band to one side of the steering wheel. It hung there like a fool's balloon, bobbing lightly away if I touched it.

I had been thirsty all day, but not unbearably.

After dark, some hovering internal rumbles identified themselves as hunger. Again, not unbearably.

The bladder problem reappeared and was again a disaster. But time, I supposed, would lessen the difficulty: no input, less output.

Hope had to be filed under "Pending," after dark. Twelve hours to be lived before one could climb onto the will-they won't-they treadmill again. I found the hours long, lonely, and dreadful.

The cramps which I had so imaginatively constructed for the film began to afflict my body in earnest once the heat of the day drained away and let my muscles grow stiff.

At first, I warmed up by another dozen wrenching attempts to break the steering wheel off the control column, the net result of which was considerable wear and tear on me, and none on the car. After that, I tried to plan a sensible series of isometric exercises which would keep everything warm and working, but I only got about half of them done.

Against all the odds, I went to sleep.

The nightmare was still there when I woke up.

I was shivering with cold, creakingly stiff, and perceptibly hungrier.

I had nothing to eat but four matches, a handkerchief, and a blunt pencil.

After a small amount of thought, I dug out the pencil and chewed that. Not exactly for the food value, but to bare the lead. With that pencil, I decided, I could bring Danilo down.

Before dawn, the realization crept slowly in that Danilo could not have abandoned me in the car without help. He would have needed someone to drive him away when he had finished locking me in. He wouldn't have walked through the game reserve, not only because of the danger from animals but because a man on foot would have been as conspicuous as gallantry.

So someone had helped him.

Who?

Arknold . . .

He had shut his eyes to Danilo's fraud when he had discovered it: had kept silent, because by not arranging better security he had put his license at risk. But would he step deep into murder to save himself a suspension?

No. He wouldn't.

Barty, for money?

I didn't know.

One—any—of the van Hurens, for any reason at all?

No.

Roderick, for news? Or Katya, or Melanie.

No.

Clifford Wenkins, for publicity?

If it was him, I was safe, because he wouldn't leave me there much longer. He wouldn't dare. Worldic, for a start, wouldn't want the merchandise turning up in a damaged state. I wished I believed it was Wenkins, but I didn't.

Evan? Conrad?
I couldn't face it.
They had both been there. On the spot. Sleeping next door. Handy for breaking in in the night and smothering me with ether.
One of them could have done it while the other slept. But which? And why?

If it was either Evan or Conrad, I was going to die, because only they could save me.

The dawn came up on this bleakest of thoughts and showed me that my theories on water vapor were correct. I could see nothing of the Kruger National Park, because all the windows were fogged and beaded with condensation.
I could reach the glass beside me, and I licked it. It felt great. The dryness of my tongue and throat became instantly less aggravating, though I could still have done with a pint of draught.
I looked through the licked patch. Same old wilderness. Same old no one there.
My spoonful of water had formed all right inside the now cold plastic bag. Carefully I loosened its neck in the rubber band and squeezed the shrunken air out, to prevent it expanding again when the day grew hot, and reabsorbing the precious liquid. I wouldn't drink it until later, I decided. Until things got worse.

With all the precious humidity clinging to the inside of the windows, it was safe to embark on a change of air. I took off my sock and turned the handle with my toes, and opened the left-hand window a scant inch. Couldn't risk not being able to shut it again; but when the sun came up I got it shut without much trouble. When the growing heat cleared the windows by re-evaporating the water, at least I had such comfort as there was in knowing it was all still inside the car, doing its best.

The pencil I had chewed in the night (and stowed for safe storage under my watch strap) was showing signs of usefulness. One more session with the incisors, and it had enough bare lead at the tip for me to write with.

The only thing to write on that I had in my pockets was the inside of the book of matches, which was room enough for "Danilo did it," but not for my whole purpose. There were maps and car documents, however, in the glove compartment in front of the passenger seat, and after a long struggle, tying my toes in knots and using up a great deal too much precious energy, I collected into my hands a large brown envelope, and a book of maps with nice blank end papers.

There was a lot to write.

15

Danilo had suggested to Nerissa that I go to South Africa because there, far from home, he could take or make any opportunity that offered to bring me to an accidental-looking death. He had lured me to the killing ground with a bait he knew I would take—a near-dying request from a woman I liked and was grateful to.

A death which was clearly a murder would have left him too dangerously exposed as a suspect. An obvious accident would bo less suspiciously investigated—like a live microphone.

Danilo hadn't been there, in Randfontein House.

Roderick had been there, and Clifford Wenkins, and Conrad. And fifty others besides. If Danilo had provided the live mike, someone at the press interview must have steered it into my hands. Luck alone had taken it out again.

Down the mine, at the suddenly opportune moment—bash.

Except for the steadfastness of a checker called Nyembezi, that attempt would have come off.

This wouldn't look like a natural accident, though. The handcuffs couldn't be called accidental.

Perhaps Danilo intended to come back after I was dead, and take them away. Perhaps people would believe then that I had lost my way in the park and had died in the car rather than risk walking.

But the time span was tight. He couldn't wait a week to make sure I was dead before coming back, because by then everyone would be searching for me, and someone might have reached me before he did.

I sighed dispiritedly.

None of it made any sense.

The day proved an inferno compared with the one before. Much worse even than Spain. The scorching fury of the heat stunned me to the point where thought became impossible, and cramps racked my shoulders, arms, and stomach.

I tucked my hands into my sleeves and rolled my head back out of the direct rays and just sat there enduring it, because there was nothing else to do.

So much for my pathetic little attempts at water management. The brutal sun was shriveling me minute by minute, and I knew that a week was wildly optimistic. In this heat, a day or two would be enough.

My throat burned with thirst, and saliva was a thing of the past.

A gallon of water in the car's radiator ... as out of reach as a mirage.

When I couldn't swallow without wincing or breathe without feeling the intaken air cut like a knife, I untied the plastic bag and poured the contents into my mouth. I made the divine H_2O last as long as possible; rolled it round my teeth and gums, and under my tongue. There was hardly enough left to swallow, and when it was gone I felt wretched. There was nothing now between me and nightfall.

I turned the bag inside out and sucked it, and held it against my mouth until the heat had dried it entirely, and then I filled it again with hot air, and with trembling fingers fumbled it back into the rubber band on the steering wheel.

I remembered that the boot of the car still held, as far as I knew, a lot of oddments of Conrad's equipment. Surely he would need it, would come looking for that, if not for me.

Evan, I thought, for God's sake come and find me.

But Evan had gone north in the park, which stretched two hundred miles to the boundary on the great gray-green greasy Limpopo River. Evan was searching there for his Elephant's Child.

And I . . . I was sitting in a car, dying for a gold mine I didn't want.

Night came, and hunger.

People paid to be starved in Health Farms, and people went on hunger strikes to protest about this or that, so what was so special about hunger?

Nothing. It was just a pain.

The night was cool, was blessed. In the morning, when I had licked as much of the window as I could reach, I went on with the writing. I wrote everything I could think of which would help an investigation into my death.

The heat started up before I had finished. I wrote, "Give my love to Charlie," and signed my name, because I wasn't certain that by that evening I would be able to write any more. Then I slid the written papers under my left thigh so that they wouldn't slip out of reach on the floor, and tucked the little pencil under my watch strap, and collapsed the air out of the plastic bag to keep the next teaspoonful safe, and wondered how long, how long I would last.

By midday, I didn't want to last.

I held out until then for my sip of water, but when it was gone I would have been happy to die. After the bag had dried against my face, it took a very long time, and a great effort of will, for me to balloon it out and fix it again to the steering wheel. Tomorrow, I thought, the thimbleful would form again, but I would be past drinking it.

We had been wrong in the film, I thought. We had focused on the mental state of the man too much, to the neglect of the physical. We hadn't known about legs like lead and ankles swollen to giant puffballs. I had long ago shed my socks, and would have had as much chance of forcing my shoes on again as of flying.

We hadn't known the abdomen would become agonizingly distended with gas, or that the seat belts would strain across it like hawsers. We hadn't guessed that the eyes would feel like sandpaper when the lachrymal glands dried up. We had underestimated what dehydration did to the throat.

The overwhelming heat battered all emotion into numbness. There was nothing anywhere but pain, and no prospect that it would stop.

Except, of course, in death.

In the late afternoon, an elephant came and uprooted the tree the giraffe had browsed from.

That should be allegorical enough for Evan, I thought confusedly. Elephants were the indestructible destroyers of the wilderness.

But Evan was miles away.

Evan, I thought, Evan ... Oh, God, Evan ... come ... and find me.

The elephant ate a few succulent leaves off the tree and went away and left it with its roots in the air, dying for lack of water.

Before dark, I did write a few more sentences. My hands trembled continually, and folded into tight cramps, and in the end were too weak to hold the pencil.

It fell down on the floor and rolled beneath my seat. I couldn't see it, or pick it up with my swollen toes.

Weeping would have been a waste of water.

Night came again and time began to blur.

I couldn't remember how long I had been there, or how long it was until Wednesday.

Wednesday was as far away as Charlie, and I wouldn't see either of them. I had a vision of the pool in the garden with the kids splashing in it, and it was the car that seemed unreal, not the pool.

Tremors shook my limbs for hours on end.

The night was cold. Muscles stiffened. Teeth chattered. Stomach shrieked to be fed.

In the morning, the condensation on the windows was so heavy that water trickled in rivulets down the glass. I could only, as ever, reach the small area near my head. I licked it weakly. It wasn't enough.

I hadn't the energy any more to open the window for a change of air; but cars were never entirely airtight, and it wouldn't be asphyxiation that saw me off.

The inevitable sun came back in an innocent rosy dawn, gentle prelude to the terrifying day ahead.

I no longer believed that anyone would come.

All that remained was to suffer into unconsciousness, because after that there would be peace. Even delirium would be a sort of peace, because the worst torment was to be aware, to understand. I would welcome a clouded mind, when it came. That, for me, would be the real death. The only one that mattered. I wouldn't know or care when my heart finally stopped.

Heat bullied into the car like a battering ram.

I burned.

I burned.

16

They did come.

When the sun was high, Evan and Conrad came in the station wagon: Evan stampeding about in a frenzy of energy, waving his arms about, with his hair sticking out crazily and his eyes too hot for comfort; Conrad, puffing slightly under the droopy mustache, mopping his forehead with a handkerchief.

They simply walked up to the car and opened the door. Then they stood still. And stared.

I thought they were unreal; the onset of delusion. I stared back, waiting for them to vanish.

Then Evan said, "Where the hell have you been? We've been searching the whole bloody park for you since yesterday morning."

I didn't answer him. I couldn't.

Conrad was saying, "My God, my God, dear boy, my God . . ." as if the needle had stuck.

Evan went back to the station wagon, drove it across the grass, and parked it alongside the car I was in. Then he scrambled into the back and unclipped the red thermal box.

"Will beer do?" he shouted. "We didn't bring any water."

Beer would do.

He poured it from the can into a plastic cup and held it to my mouth. It was cold, alive, incredible. I drank only half, because it hurt to swallow.

Conrad opened the left-hand door and sat on the seat beside me.

"We haven't a key for the handcuffs," he said apologetically.

A laugh twitched somewhere inside me, the first for a long time.

"Phew," Evan said. "You do stink."

They saw I couldn't talk. Evan poured more beer into the cup and held it for me, and Conrad got out of the car and rummaged about in the boot. He came back with four short lengths of strong wire and a roll of insulating tape, and with these he proceeded to set me free.

He stuck the four wires into the barrel of the handcuff lock, bound the protruding ends tightly together to give a handle for leverage, and began to turn. The makeshift key did a grand job. With a lot of swearing and a couple of fresh starts when the wires slipped out, Conrad got the cuff on my right wrist opened.

And who cared about the other? It could wait.

They unclipped the seat belts and tried to help me out of the car, but I had been sitting in the same restricted position for over eighty hours and, like concrete, my body seemed to have set in the mold.

Evan said doubtfully, "I think one of us should go and find a doctor."

I shook my head decidedly. There were things I wanted to tell them before the outside world broke in. I felt jerkily under my thigh for the papers I had written, and made writing motions with my hands. Conrad silently produced the gold ball-point he always carried, and I shakily wrote on an unused corner of brown envelope, *If you do not tell anyone you have found me, we can catch the man who put me here."* And, as an afterthought, I added, *"I want to do that."*

They read the uneven words and stood wondering, almost literally scratching their heads.

I wrote a bit more. *"Please put something over the windscreen."*

That at least made sense to them. Conrad draped the front of the car with a heavy groundsheet which effectively brought the temperature down by ten degrees.

Evan saw the plastic bag hanging from the steering wheel and pulled it off its rubber band.

"What the hell is this?" he said.

I pointed to the still undrunk mouthful of water lurking in one corner. Evan understood, and looked completely appalled.

He took the written pages out of my hand, and read them. I drank some more beer, holding the cup with trembly fingers but feeling life flowing back through all the dying channels with every difficult swallow.

He read right to the end and handed the pages to Conrad. He stared at me with stunned speechlessness. An unaccustomed state for Evan. After a long time, he said slowly, "Did you really think Conrad or I had helped to leave you here?"

I shook my head.

"And you can cross off poor old Clifford Wenkins, too, because he's dead. They fished him out of the Wemmer Pan on Saturday afternoon. He went boating, and drowned."

The news took a while to percolate. I thought, No more stuttering, no more damp palms, no more nervous little man . . . poor little nervous man. . . .

I lifted Conrad's golden pen, and Evan gave me one of his ubiquitous notebooks to write on.

"I'd like to lie down. In the station wagon?"

"Sure," he said, seeming to be glad of an excuse for activity. "We'll make you a bed."

He hopped into the station wagon again and hauled all their equipment to one side. In the cleared space, he constructed a mattress from the back seats of both cars, and made a thick pillow out of coats and sweaters.

"The Ritz," he said, "is at your service."

I tried a smile and caught sight of it in the driving mirror.

Ghastly. I had a four-day beard and sunken pinkish eyes, and looked as gray and red as a sunburned ghost.

With more gentleness than I would have thought either of them had in their natures, they helped me out of the car and carried more than supported me over to the station wagon. Bent double, creaking in every muscle, and feeling that my lumbar vertebrae were breaking, I completed the journey and, once lying in the makeshift bed, began the luxuriously painful process of straightening myself out. Evan took the groundsheet off my car and spread it over the roof of the station wagon, as much to shut out the heat as for shade.

I wrote again. *"Stay here, Evan,"* because I thought they might start my car with a jump lead, and drive off for help. He looked doubtful, so I added with a fair amount of desperation, *"Please don't leave me."*

"Christ," he said when he read that. "Christ, mate, we won't leave you." He was clearly emotionally upset, which surprised me. He didn't even like me, and in the Special had heaped on the discomfort without mercy.

I drank some more beer, mouthful by separate mouthful. My throat still beat a raging case of tonsillitis out of sight, but the lubrication was slowly taking effect. I could move my tongue better, and it was beginning to feel less like a swollen lump of liver.

Evan and Conrad sat in the front seats of the station wagon and began discussing where to go. They had no accommodation reserved at Skukusa, which it appeared was still the nearest camp, and it was two hours' drive to the beds booked at Satara.

Satara and the beds won, which seemed good enough for me.

Evan said, "We might as well get going, then. It's too bloody hot here. I've had enough of it. We'll find a patch of decent shade along the road, and stop for lunch. It's after two already, and I'm hungry."

That was a lot more like the Evan I knew and detested. With an inward smile, I had another go with the pen.

"Remember how to get back here."

"Someone else can fetch the car," said Evan impatiently. "Later."

I shook my head. *"We must come back."*

"Why?"

"To catch Danilo Cavesey."

They looked from the pad to my face. Then Evan merely said, "How?"

I wrote down how. They read it. The air of excited intensity reawoke in Evan, and rapid professional calculations furrowed Conrad's forehead, for what I was asking them to do was much to their liking. Then a separate, secondary thought struck both of them, and they looked at me doubtfully.

"You can't mean it, dear boy," Conrad said.

I nodded.

"What about the person who helped him?" Evan asked. "What are you going to do about him?"

"He's dead now."

"Dead?" He looked incredulous. "You don't mean ... Clifford Wenkins?"

I nodded. I was tired. I wrote, *"Tell you when I can talk."*

They agreed to that. They shut the doors of my car, climbed into the front seat of the station wagon, turned it around, and set off along the dirt road which had for so long been for me just a reflection in a three- by six-inch looking glass.

Conrad drove, and Evan made a map. They seemed to have found me by the merest chance, as I had been a mile up a side branch of an equally unkempt road leading to a now dry water hole. The water-hole road joined into another, which led finally back to the roads used by visitors. Evan said he could find the way straight back to my car; it was easy. They had searched, he added, every side road they could find between Skukusa and Numbi, and that had been yesterday. Today they had tried the dry sparse land to the south of the Sabie River, and they had found me on the fifth "No Entry" they had explored.

After five or six miles, we came to a small group of trees throwing some dappled shade. Conrad at once pulled in and stopped the car, and Evan without more ado started burrowing into the red box. They had brought more sandwiches, more fruit, more beer.

I thought I would postpone sandwiches and fruit. Beer was doing wonders. I drank some more.

The other two munched away as if the whole picnic were routine. They opened the windows wide, reckoning that any sensible animal would be sleeping in this heat, not looking out for unwary humans.

No cars passed. Every sensible human, too, was busy at siesta in the air-conditioned camps. Evan, of course, was impervious to heat, and Conrad had to lump it.

I wrote again. *"What made you start looking for me?"*

Evan spoke round bits of ham sandwich. "We kept wanting the things of Conrad's that were in your car. It became most annoying not to have them. So yesterday morning we telephoned the Iguana to tell you how selfish you had been to take them away with you."

"They said you weren't there," Conrad said. "They said they understood you were going to the Kruger Park for several days."

"We couldn't understand it," Evan said, nodding. "In view of your note."

"What note?" I tried automatically to say the words, but my throat still wouldn't have it. I wrote them instead.

"The note you left," Evan said impatiently, "saying you had gone back to Johannesburg."

"I left no note."

He stopped chewing and sat with his mouth full, as if in suspended animation. Then he took up chewing again and said, "No. That's right. You couldn't have."

"We thought you had, anyway," Conrad said. "It was just a piece of paper, written in capital letters, saying,

'Gone back to Johannesburg. Link.' Bloody rude and un-grateful, dear boy, we thought it. Packing all your gear and buzzing off at the crack of dawn without even bother-ing to say goodbye."

"Sorry."

Conrad laughed. "After that, we tried to reach Clifford Wenkins, because we thought he might know where you were, but all we got at his number was some hysterical woman saying he'd been drowned in the Wemmer Pan."

"We tried one or two other people," Evan went on. "The van Hurens, and so on."

"Danilo?" I wrote.

"No." Evan shook his head. "Didn't think of him. Wouldn't know where he's staying, for a start." He ate a mouthful, reflecting. "We thought it a bit unhelpful of you to go off without letting anyone know where you could be found, and then we thought perhaps you'd been damn bloody careless and got lost in the park, and never got back to Johannesburg at all. So after a bit of argy-bargy we persuaded the reception office at Satara to check what time you went out to the Numbi gate on Friday morning, and the gatekeeper said that according to their records you hadn't gone out at all."

"We telephoned Haagner, dear boy," Conrad said, "and explained the situation, but he didn't seem to be much worried. He said people often talked their way out of Numbi without papers, even though one was supposed to produce receipts to show one had paid for staying in camps. Mr. Lincoln would only have to say, Haagner said, that Evan and Conrad were still in the park, and had paid for him. The Numbi men would check with Skukusa, and then let Mr. Lincoln go. He also said you couldn't be lost in the park. You were too sensible, he said, and only fools got lost. People who drove miles down no-entry roads and then had their cars break down."

And that, I presumed, was what they thought had hap-pened. But I wouldn't grumble.

They opened cans of beer and gulped. I went on sip-ping.

"We had sure enough paid for you at Skukusa," Evan said accusingly. "Including the window you broke."

I only had to pick up the pen.

"My God," Evan said before I got it to the paper. "Danilo Cavesey broke the window . . . to get into your rondavel."

I supposed so. He had got past the locked door without waking me.

"You're a fairly valuable property, dear boy," Conrad said, finishing the saga. "So we decided we ought perhaps to spend a day or so looking for you."

"We saw a splendid herd of elephants yesterday afternoon," said Evan, pointing out that the delay to their original plans had not been an entire waste. "And we might see some more today," he said.

They helped me into the rondavel in Satara and I asked them to turn the air conditioning off, as to me the hut felt cold. If I got cold again, I would get stiff again, which would only add to my aches. I lay on one of the beds with three blankets over me and felt lousy.

Conrad fetched a glass of water, and he and Evan stood around looking helpless.

Evan said, "Let's take your stinking clothes off. You'd embarrass a pig as you are."

I shook my head.

"If we bring you some water, would you like to wash?"

No, again.

Evan wrinkled his nose. "Well, you won't mind if neither of us sleeps in here with you?"

I shook my head. My smell was offensive to myself as well, now that I'd breathed so much clean fresh air.

Conrad went off to the camp shop to find something I could swallow, and presently came back with a pint of milk and a tin of chicken soup. The only opener they had was the beer-can opener, but they got the soup out into a jug in the end. There was nothing to heat the soup with, so they tipped in half the milk and stirred it around until it was runny. Then they poured out a glassful, and, grateful for their clumsy care, I drank it bit by bit.

"Now," said Evan briskly, satisfied that they had done the best possible for me, "let's get on with planning the trap."

This time, when I tried, some semblance of speech came out.

"Danilo is staying at the Vaal Majestic," I said.

"What did you say?" Evan demanded. "Thank God you can talk again, but I couldn't understand a word of it."

I wrote it down.

"Oh. Right."

I said, "Telephone in the morning, and tell him . . " It was a croak, rough and cracked.

"Look," Evan interrupted, "we'll get along quicker if you write it."

I nodded. Much easier on my throat, if he preferred it that way.

"At breakfast time, tell Danilo you are trying to find out where I am because I have Conrad's equipment in my car. Tell him I also have Conrad's gold pencil in my pocket, and he especially wants it back. Tell him I also have one of your notebooks, and you need your notes. Tell him you are worried because I had some theory that someone I knew had been trying to kill me."

Evan read, and looked dubious. "Are you sure that will bring him?"

I wrote: *"Would you risk my being able to write down that theory if you knew I had pencil and paper within reach?"*

He considered. He said, "No. I wouldn't."

"I did do it."

"So you did."

Conrad sat heavily down in the armchair, nodding.

"What next, dear boy?"

I wrote: *"This evening, telephone Quentin van Huren. Tell him where and in what state you found me. Say I wrote some notes. Read them to him. Tell him about the trap for Danilo. Ask him to tell the police. With his authority, he can arrange it properly."*

"Sure. Sure." Evan, with undaunted wiry energy, collected up my writings from the car and his notebook with all our plans, and strode off at once to the telephone in the main building.

Conrad stayed behind and lit a cigar, no doubt to fend off evil odors.

"It was Evan who insisted on looking for you, dear boy," he said. "Absolutely fanatical, he was. You know how he never lets up when he gets an idea. We went up every unlikely track—bloody silly, I thought—until we found you."

"Who," I said slowly, trying to speak clearly, "told Danilo about the film . . . *Man in a Car?"*

He shrugged a little uncomfortably. "Maybe I did. At Germiston. They were all asking about your latest work—the van Hurens, Clifford Wenkins, Danilo—everybody."

It didn't matter. Wenkins could have got hold of the film's plot easily enough, through Worldic.

"Dear boy," Conrad said thoughtfully. "The make-up is all wrong in the film." He puffed the cigar. "Mind you," he said, "what you actually look like would be pretty poor box office."

"Thanks."

He smiled. "Have some more soup?"

Evan was gone a long time and came back looking earnest and intense.

"He wants me to ring back later. He was pretty incoherent when I'd finished." Evan raised his eyebrows, surprised that anyone should need time to assimilate so many unwelcome facts. "He said he would think over what ought to be done. And—oh, yes, he said to ask you why you now thought it was Clifford Wenkins who helped Danilo."

I said, "Clifford Wenkins would have helped—"

"Write it down," said Evan impatiently. "You sound like a crow with laryngitis."

I wrote: *"Clifford Wenkins would do anything for publicity stunts. He would exchange recording gear and microphones for instance. I do not believe he thought anyone would be killed, but if I got an electric shock at a press conference, it would put my name and the purpose of my visit in the papers. I believe Danilo put it all into his head, and gave him the live equipment. Wenkins was terrified when Katya was so badly shocked, and afterwards I saw him telephoning, looking very worried. I thought he was calling Worldic, but he might have been telling Danilo that the stunt had gone wrong."*

"It went better, dear boy, from Worldic's point of view," Conrad commented.

"Worldic drove Clifford Wenkins unmercifully to arrange publicity stunts, so if Danilo suggested to him that they should kidnap me and lock me in a car, just like in my new film, he would have been foolish enough to agree.

"When I'd been in the car for three days, I did not think it could be Wenkins who'd been helping Danilo, because I knew Wenkins would not leave me there very long. But once Wenkins was dead, no one but Danilo knew where I was. He had only to leave me there.

"After my body was discovered, people would work out that it had been a publicity stunt planned by Wenkins and myself, which went wrong because he drowned and could not set in motion the necessary search.

"I expect it was in Wenkins' car that he and Danilo drove into the park, so that the Numbi gate office would have it on record that he had been there."

Evan practically tore the notebook out of my hands, as he had been striding around with impatience while I wrote. He read to the end and handed the notebook to Conrad.

"Do you realize," he demanded, "that you are practically accusing Danilo of killing Clifford Wenkins so that you shouldn't be found?"

I nodded.

"I think he did," I croaked. "For a gold mine."

They left me with water and soup to hand and went off to dinner in the restaurant. When they came back, Evan had telephoned again to van Huren.

"He'd grasped everything a bit better," Evan allowed condescendingly. "I read him what you wrote about Wenkins, and he said he thought you could be right. He said he was upset about Danilo, because he had liked him, but he would do as you asked. He said that he himself would come down here. He's flying down to the Skukusa airstrip first thing in the morning. The police will be properly genned up. Conrad and I will meet them and van Huren at Skukusa, and go on from there, if it looks likely that Danilo has taken the bait."

We were going to call Danilo in the morning. Even if he, too, flew down as fast as possible, everyone should be in position before he came.

The night was paradise compared with its predecessors, but still far short of heaven. In the morning, I felt a good deal stronger: there were no more cramps and the fire in my throat would no longer frighten Celsius. I got myself to the bathroom looking as bent as old Adam the gardener, but I got there; and I ate the banana which Conrad brought me for breakfast.

Evan had gone to telephone Danilo, Conrad said, and Evan came later with a satisfied smile.

"He was there," he said. "And I'd say there was no doubt he swallowed it. He sounded pretty worried—sharp voice, that sort of thing. He asked why I was so sure about the gold pencil. Can you believe it? I said Conrad had lent it to you Thursday evening and I'd seen you put it in your pocket. Then, Friday morning, you went off to Johannesburg without giving it back."

17

       The hardest thing I ever did was to get back into that car.

We reached it at half past ten, and Evan and Conrad busily rigged up various bits and pieces, including a warning buzzer which would tell me when Danilo was approaching.

Half an hour later, when they had finished, the day was stoking up to another roaster. I drank the whole of the bottle of water we had brought from Satara and ate another banana.

Evan danced up and down. "Come on. Come on. We haven't got all day. We've got to hurry to Skukusa to meet van Huren."

I left the station wagon, hobbled across to the car, sat in the front seat, and fastened the seat belts.

The dying aches flared up at once.

Conrad approached with the handcuffs, and my throat closed. I couldn't look at him, couldn't look at Evan ... at anything. Couldn't do it ... all my nerves and muscles revolted.

Couldn't.

Conrad, watching me, said practically, "You haven't got to, Link. It's your own idea, dear boy. He will come, whether you are here or not."

"Don't try and dissuade him," Evan said crossly. "Not now we've gone to all this trouble. And as Link pointed out himself, if he isn't in the car when Danilo comes, nothing will be conclusive."

Conrad still hesitated. My fault.

"Get on with it," Evan said.

I put my arm through the steering wheel. It was trembling.

Conrad clicked the handcuffs shut first on one wrist and then the other, and I shuddered from head to foot.

"Dear boy . . ." Conrad said doubtfully.

"Come on," Evan urged.

I didn't say anything. I thought that whatever I might start to say would come out as a screaming plea that they wouldn't leave me. Leave me, however, they must.

Evan shut the car door brusquely, and jerked his head for Conrad to follow him into the station wagon. Conrad went with his head turned backward, looking to see if I was calling him.

They climbed into the front seat, turned, and drove away. The silence of the tinder-dry park settled around me.

I wished I had never suggested this plan. The car seemed hotter than ever, the heat more intolerable. Within an hour, and in spite of the quantities of water I had drunk that morning, fierce thirst returned.

Cramps began again in my legs. My spine protested. My shoulders pulled with strain.

I cursed myself.

Supposing he took all day, I thought. Supposing he didn't fly down, but drove. Eight o'clock, when Evan telephoned him. At least five hours' drive to Numbi, another hour and a half to reach me. . . . He might not come until three or four, which meant five hours in the car. . . .

I tucked my hands into my shirt sleeves and stretched my head back out of the sun.

There was no water vapor, no plastic bag, to keep my mind occupied. The pencil-written sheets lay on my knees, with Conrad's gold pencil, companion to his pen, clipping them together. There was no leaping from hope to despair and back again, which was certainly a blessed relief, but unexpectedly left too much time free for pure feeling.

Every minute dragged.

The première, I thought, was due to be held the following night. I wondered who would be arranging everything, with poor Clifford Wenkins in his watery grave. I wondered if I would get to the Klipspringer Heights Hotel on time. In another twenty-four hours, shaved, bathed, rested, watered, and fed, perhaps I might just make it. All those people paying twenty rand for a seat . . . unfair not to turn up, if I could. . . .

Time crawled. I looked at my watch. It wasn't trying.
One o'clock came. One o'clock went.
Conrad had fixed a radio transmitter with a button for me to press if I simply could not stand any more. But if I pressed it, the whole of today's effort would be wasted. If I pressed it, the cohorts would rush to my rescue, but Danilo would see the activity and would never come near.

I wished Conrad hadn't insisted on that button. Evan said it was necessary so that he and van Huren and the police would know for certain that Danilo had come, if they should by some chance miss him on the road.

One buzz was to mean that Danilo had come.
Two buzzes that he had left again.
A series of short buzzes would bring them instantly at any time to set me free.

I would wait another ten minutes before I gave up, I thought.
Then another ten.
Then another.
Ten minutes was always possible.

Conrad's warning buzzer sounded like a wasp in my ear and jerked me into action.

Danilo drove up beside me and stopped where the station wagon had been.

I pressed the buttons taped within reach on the steering column.

I put all the actor's art I had into looking not far from death, and didn't have to elaborate all that much on what I knew of the real thing. A couple of vultures had conveniently flapped and spiraled down, and now perched on a nearby tree like brooding anarchists awaiting the revolution. I eyed them sourly, but Danilo was reassured.

He opened the door, and through slit eyes I saw him draw back when the unmitigated heat-stoked stench met his nostrils. It had been worth not washing, not changing my clothes. There was nothing about me to show I hadn't sat in that spot continuously since he had left me there, and a great deal to prove I had.

He looked at my lolling head, my flaccid hands, my bare swollen feet. He showed no remorse whatever. The sun blazed on the bright blond head, giving him a halo. The clean-featured all-American boy, as shiny, cold, and ruthless as ice.

He bent down and practically snatched the papers off my lap. Unclipped the pencil and threw it on the back seat of the car. Read what I had written, right to the end.

"So you did guess . . . you did write," he said. "Clever Ed Lincoln, too clever by half. Too bad no one will ever read this. . . ." He peered down into my half-shut eyes to make sure I could hear him, could see him. Then he took a cigarette lighter, flicked the flint, and set the corners of the papers into the flame.

I shook feebly in my seat, in mute protest. It pleased him. He smiled.

He turned the papers, burning them all up, and then ground the ashes into just more dust in the dusty grass.

"There," he said cheerfully.

I made a small croak. He paid attention.

I said, "Let . . . me . . . go."

"Not a chance." He put his hand in his pocket and brought out a bunch of keys. "Keys to the car." He held them up, jingling. "Key to the handcuffs." He waved it in front of my eyes.

"Please," I said.

"You're worth too much to me dead, pal. Sorry and all that. But there it is."

He put the keys in his pocket, shut the door on me, and without another glance, drove heartlessly away.

Poor Nerissa, I thought. I hoped she would die before she found out about Danilo; but life was not always kind.

In time, four cars rolled back into the reflection in the driving mirror, and stopped in a cluster round my car. Evan and Conrad's station wagon. A chauffeur-driven car with van Huren. Two police cars: the first containing, I later discovered, their photographer and their surgeon; the second, three senior police officers and Danilo Cavesey.

They all stood up outside the cars: a meal and a half for any passing pride of lion. Wild animals, however, kept decently out of sight. Danilo outdid them all for savagery.

Conrad bustled over and pulled open the door.

"You all right, dear boy?" he said anxiously.

I nodded.

Danilo was saying loudly and virtuously, "I told you, I'd just found him, and I was driving away to get help."

"Oh, yeah," Conrad muttered, digging out his bits of wire.

"He has the key of the handcuffs in his pocket," I said.

"You don't mean it, dear boy?" He saw I did mean it. He went over and told the police, and after a short scuffle they found the key. Also the car keys. And now perhaps Mr. Cavesey would explain why he was driving away when he had in his pocket the means of freeing Mr. Lincoln?

Mr. Cavesey glowered and declined. He had been going for help, he said.

Evan, enjoying himself immensely, walked over to the tree the elephant had uprooted, and from its withering foliage disentangled the Arriflex on its tripod.

"Everything you did here, we filmed," he told Danilo. "Link had a cable to the car. He started the camera when you arrived."

Conrad fished his best tape recorder out from under the car and unhitched the sensitive microphone from just inside the door frame.

"Everything you said here," he echoed, with equal satisfaction, "we recorded. Link switched on the recorder when you came."

The police produced a pair of handcuffs of their own, and put them on Danilo, who had gone blue-white under the suntan.

Quentin van Huren walked over to the car and looked down at me. Conrad had forgotten the small detail of bringing back the key to free me. I still sat, locked and helpless, where I had begun.

"For God's sake . . ." Van Huren looked appalled.

I smiled lopsidedly and shook my head. "For gold's sake," I said.

His mouth moved, but no words came out.

Gold, greed, and gilded boys—a thoroughly bad mixture.

Evan was strutting around looking important, intense, and satisfied, as if he had stage-managed and directed the entire performance. But he saw that I was still tethered, and for once some twitch of compassion reached him. He went to fetch the handcuffs key and brought it over.

He stood beside van Huren for a second, staring down at me as if seeing something new. For the first time ever, he smiled with a hint of friendship.

"Cut," he said. "No retakes today."